ruck me harder

Neurospicy Book Club
Book Three

allie lasky

 Formatted with Vellum

one

. . .

Viv

FUCK. My head hurts.

As I roll over, my body twinges with the ache of exertion. I can hardly breathe. My head is pounding so hard. My mouth tastes like sawdust and between my legs feels—

My eyes fly open. No. Please tell me I didn't…

Lifting the comforter, I confirm that yes, I'm naked, and the telltale slickness and ache between my legs tells me exactly what I got up to last night.

Did he…

Turning my head, I confirm what I already expected. He's gone. Whoever he is, he's long gone, and the bed beside me is cool. I don't know if I'm relieved or upset. The twin frame probably couldn't hold both of us, anyway. I'm barely able to fit on the small dorm bed on my own.

There's a condom wrapper in the trashcan beside the bed, so clearly, we were safe. Good. That's one less thing to worry about.

With a groan, I force myself upright. My roommate is asleep. She can sleep through a tornado siren, something we learned when we were in Iowa for an exhibition game a few years ago. I can only hope she was asleep—or better yet, not in the room—when I got down with whoever I got down with.

He was cute. I remember that. About my height, with shaggy, dark hair and dark eyes. Clean cut. Muscles for days. Covered in ink.

Someone on the volleyball team snuck in the booze. Strictly speaking, alcohol isn't allowed in the Olympic Village, but now at my second Games, I'm seeing all the ways the rules are broken. We also aren't supposed to invite other countries into the dormitories, but France and Brazil were definitely partying with us in Japan's territory last week.

Being at the Olympics is nothing like I expected. When I pictured my return to the Games, my quest for redemption, I thought I'd find meaning and fulfillment in playing my heart out.

It's not enough.

We have the finals tomorrow against Australia. They were our downfall four long years ago. I can still hear the taunting.

It doesn't help that two of my teammates back home are Aussies. Sure, I love them when we're on the same team, but staring at me from across the pitch, they're the enemy.

And tomorrow, they are going down.

But first—a shower.

———

Rugby has brought me intense joy and satisfaction. For the last decade, I've worked my ass off—for the league, for the national federation. For me.

Tomorrow starts my last season. Well—training camp. After the season ends, either I have another Olympic berth or I don't. Either way, I'm done. My body can't handle much more.

Rugby is a spring sport with a fall training season. The sevens season in the summer this year will be the Olympics instead. I've given rugby my all since I was eighteen years old, and now at twenty-nine, I think I'm entitled to take some time off.

My agent would probably love for me to keep going, keep playing, but Alycia knows as well as I do that my body is starting to fail. The endorsement campaigns are starting to slow down. Not that there were all that many to begin with. The entire pie of endorsement options is small, and when you cut slivers off for the young, cute players with sunny personalities, the new pseudo-influencers, and the new girls coming onto the squad... Nobody's going to look twice at the grumpy, geriatric team captain.

It would help if I smiled more, at least that's what Alycia told me once. I scowled at her and she laughed. Yeah, I'm not a sunshine-y, happy-go-lucky sort. Not like my younger sister.

I'm a little rough around the edges. I've been to media training. It didn't stick. I can't pretend to be someone I'm not.

There's nothing *wrong* with me. I had an idyllic childhood, even if we moved around a lot. My parents are still together, still disgustingly in love. My siblings are assholes, yeah, but they love me.

Trust is a hard thing to give. It's even more difficult to receive. Unconditional love and support? I about break into hives. With my teammates though? It's easier.

As I walk into the restaurant where we're meeting, it's like a weight has been lifted from my shoulders. I'm at peace with my girls in a way I've never experienced with other teams.

The Boston Revolution is one of twelve teams in the National Rugby League. When the league started with four teams a decade ago, Boston was the flagship team. It helps that the NRL corporate offices are based here. So are the U.S. Rugby National Team headquarters.

During the season, I play with the Revolution, and the rest of the time, I work out at the U.S. National Team facilities.

They give me a small stipend for housing and meals, since I don't live on the campus. The actual monthly payment for being on the national team is a pittance. If I didn't have my regular day job as the hooker on the Revolution, I wouldn't be able to survive.

I don't do it for the money. I do it for the thrill of the game.

"Hey, Cap!" Andi calls, gesturing me to the back room of the restaurant.

As I enter the room, I'm surprised most of the team is already assembled. There are about forty women on the team, plus all of our trainers and staff.

"Viv is here!" Kiana calls. "Now it's a party!"

Laughing, I let them pull me into the swarm. It's been a full six weeks since we last saw each other at the end of the sevens season.

After our last match wrapped up and we had the media postmortem, I packed up and went to visit my family in South Carolina. It's where my parents moved a few years ago when my mom got the head coaching job for Clemson's volleyball team.

Of my five siblings, only Frankie and Bradley, the two youngest, are still in college and were home for the summer break. Chuck was home for two weeks, enjoying the remnants of his summer before hockey training camp started up. Perry was in Raleigh, working his ass off in football preseason, and Janine couldn't get time away from training for a big meet in Paris next month.

There are six of us Gallagher siblings and five of us are professional athletes. Well, Frankie's technically an amateur because she's still in college and therefore eligible for an athletic scholarship, but she's already been named to the U.S. National Volleyball team, so it's just a matter of her graduation status than anything else holding her back. Only Bradley, my youngest sibling, is not involved in sports. I'm not really sure why. He always changes the subject whenever anyone brings it up.

As much as I love my family, I have to admit they *are* intense. It's why I spend as little time as possible at home. It's nice to be with them. It's even nicer to be on my own home turf.

South Carolina isn't my home. We've moved all over for my mom's job. My dad is an executive for USA Tennis, so he does most of his work from home, interspersed with travel to competitions. My home is where my family is. And while sometimes we're spread all across the country, it's nice when we get to spend time together.

The Revolution is my home too. I've been part of this squad for five years and I've loved every minute of it. These women are my family. They'd do anything for me, and me for them.

Kiana wiggles her way through the crowd to me, pushing a drink in my hand. I raise an eyebrow and she nods.

It's not a secret that I'm sober. I've never hidden it. Still, I don't like to make a big deal out of it. People get defensive when they find out I don't drink, like I'm pointing out *their* inability to moderate their alcohol intake and not like it's because I can't handle mine.

I didn't think I had a problem with alcohol. Not until the last Olympics, when I hooked up with some random dude and felt gross and used after. I don't know that I'd remember his face, I definitely don't remember his name, and that freaks me out. If something had happened—not that it did, but *if* it had—I'd be shit out of luck trying to pull the pieces of my life back together.

But I came home from the Games, I got tested, and everything was negative. Thank goodness.

Taking a sip of the fruity mocktail, I force a smile. I don't want to think about the worst day of my life.

"How was your break?" I ask Kiana.

"Good. Not long enough," she laughs.

It's hard. Yes, I get to play the sport I love. My job is to play rugby. But I also train all the fucking time, all year round. Six weeks at the end of the summer is not a real rest when I have to train the other 46.

Then again… I'm a peak athlete at the waning end of my career. I've been to two Olympics—hopefully three—and I've won the national championship twice. I've had a storybook career. I can rest when I retire. Maybe.

two

. . .

Viv

NOW THAT I'M back in the grind of pre-season prep, I remember all the reasons I fell in love with rugby. Surrounded by my teammates, working day in and day out for a bigger purpose, a bright goal…

We're going to win the national championship this year. I can feel it in my bones. I want it. I want it *bad*. I'll stop at nothing to bring the trophy back home to Boston, where it should be.

Today has been the kind of dreary fall day where the weather has a mind of its own. It's taunting me, teasing winter is on its way. Freezing cold rain. It hasn't let up all day.

As captain, it's my duty to attend all the social activities, so even though I'm not in the mood, after practice I pull myself together and show up at the pub where the team has gathered for drinks. Kiana waves at me from down the table, where she's talking to Andi and Grace. I wave back but stay where I'm at on the periphery of the group.

Cari Gonzales, the new, fresh-faced phenom out of Harvard, bounds over to me.

"Hi, Viv," she says, bubbling with enthusiasm.

"Hi." I want to be welcoming to her. She's surely going to

be an asset for our team, but right now the exuberance… it's too much.

"I just wanted to introduce myself," she says.

My eyebrows go up. I think she said that all in one breath.

"I've been a fan of yours for, like, forever," she continues. "I had a poster of you on my wall growing up. And now to be on the same team as you—wow!"

"Wow." My throat feels dry. I take a sip of my tonic water. "How old are you?"

"Twenty-two!" she chirps. "I want to get a spot on the national team this year."

"I'm sure you'll make it," I tell her. "You're insanely talented."

That's not a lie. She's one of the up-and-coming superstars in the making. College rugby is a different animal now than it was when I was in school. We're only seven years apart, but it feels like seventy.

She gapes at me. "You really think so?"

"We wouldn't have signed you if we didn't think so," I deflect.

"Can I tell you a secret?" she asks, and then before I can say anything, she continues: "I only wanted to get signed by Boston. My brothers both train here. I don't know that I'm ready to live so far away from my family."

Sidestepping that, I say, "Oh? Your brother is an athlete?"

"Both of them." She giggles. "Tony is a gymnast with the U.S. national team. He's based out of the training center in Dorchester. And Al plays for the Grizzlies."

I swallow. "Your brother is a hockey player?"

She nods, eager. "And your brother plays hockey too. We have so much in common!"

"Yeah, I guess so."

Her smile dims, likely at my disinterested tone.

Shit.

Cari is bright and sparkly. Just because I'm a jagged black

stone doesn't mean I should dim her shine. I'm not a monster, but peopling doesn't come easily to me, especially when their energy doesn't match mine. I'm a pessimist by nature; it's hard to relate to people who are naturally happy and outgoing. Once we're friends, I cherish them deeply, regardless of any personality differences. It's getting over that initial hump that's difficult for me.

Still, I don't want to be rude. She's my teammate, which means she's automatically someone whose feelings I should care about. I have to look out for her. And she's so young. My heart aches at her naiveté. She doesn't know what she's getting into with a career in professional sports.

"How are you settling in with the team?"

"It's going well!" She brightens again. "I'm having so much fun. It's a lot of work but it's the good kind of work."

I know what she means. There's nothing like the pleasant ache of sore muscles after a vigorous workout.

"Anyway," Cari says loudly. "I was talking to Al, and I was showing him some photos of the team, and he thinks you're totally gorgeous. Do you want to meet him?"

I blink. "Meet him?"

"I know blind dates are totally lame, but I promise he's a good guy," she says. "He's twenty-seven, so yeah, he's a bit younger than you, but does that really matter? He's hot too." She waggles her eyebrows.

"You think your brother is hot?" I repeat dumbly. My brain can't kick into gear.

"Not, like… No," Cari says awkwardly. "He's objectively good looking."

"Uh huh." Unable to help myself, I eye her up and down. I don't think I can keep the judgment off my face.

"I promise I'm not interested in my own brother," she blurts, her face red.

To my surprise, that cracks my mood enough that I laugh.

"I get it. My brother is, like, movie star attractive," I tell her. "Doesn't mean I want to fuck him though."

"You can fuck my brother," she offers, then winces. "I'm making this weird. I just—you're cool, and he's cool, and it would be cool if you two got together."

"And he's not just looking to hit it and quit it? I know how hockey players are."

Cari shakes her head. "He says he's over the hook up scene. Not that I want to know what my brother gets up to. You know? I don't need to know any details. He thinks you're, like, super gorgeous." She pulls out her phone. "Here. Let me show you—"

The guy on the screen is objectively cute, I guess. He has a square jaw and dark brown hair, short on the sides and longer lettuce on top, with a scruffy beard. His eyes are soulful.

From the picture, there's no tingling, no sparks, no nothing. He's just some dude.

But when I see the eagerness on my teammate's face…

"Okay, you can set us up," I relent.

He doesn't have to be Mr. Right. It's okay if he's just Mr. Right Now.

———

And that's how I find myself two weeks later on the doorstep of a small row house in Mattapan. It's not the kind of house I expected a big shot hockey star to live in. Knowing what my brother's condo and the places his friends live in back in Colorado are like…

The door swings open and Cari is on the front stoop.

"You're here!" She squeals and jumps in place. "He'll be here any minute."

"Are you sure this is a good idea?" I ask her.

"Yeah, of course!"

Al suggested something low-key, grabbing coffee and then

maybe dinner. He texted me while I was on my way that his practice was running late. Fine, okay, whatever. I get that.

He did *not* mention he lives with his sister.

I don't know why that bothers me. I lived with my brother Perry for two years when he was signed with Boston. But now…

Taking a breath, I try to release the tension in my shoulders and look around.

The house is shabby but clearly well-loved. The room is clean and smells nice. The leather couch has a plaid throw blanket tossed over the back. There are photos everywhere.

My eyes zero in on a framed photo on the wall. It's a family portrait, a young Cari and two brothers with their parents. She looks to be about fourteen, gangly and brace-faced. The brother in the middle is wearing a hockey jersey and a ball cap; he's just been drafted. The other brother is—

I swallow.

The other brother has dark hair and a short, scruffy beard. His muscles bulge in his too-small suit jacket.

But his face…

"Who's that?" I ask, pointing toward the other brother.

"Oh, that's Tony," Cari says casually.

I toss the name around. "Tony."

"Yeah. Antonio. He's the oldest," she says. "He's a gymnast."

The room starts to close in on me. The walls are shrinking. My shirt collar feels like it's choking me. I can't breathe.

"I have to go," I announce. I haven't taken my coat off yet. Good. I can make a clean break for it.

Cari frowns. "Did I do something?"

"No. This is—" I gulp. "I have to—"

She seems to read the panic on my face. "Can I get you some water?"

I shake my head. "Go. I have to go." My hands start to shake and I shove them in my pocket so she won't notice.

I can't melt down. Not here. Not now.

Cari reaches out and squeezes my arm. "Take care of yourself, Viv."

Turning to leave, I start my escape from the small living room. I'm out the door and making my way down the stairs when I run into a brick wall.

Fuck. That hurts.

Strong hands land on my biceps, steadying me.

"Are you okay?" a rough, gravelly voice asks.

I look up and recoil.

Because the wall I ran into? That's Tony Gonzales.

The guy I hooked up with at the Olympics.

The worst mistake of my life.

three

. . .

Tony

IT'S BEEN three years since I last saw Vivienne Gallagher. She was asleep in her Olympic dorm room bed, naked and sated after an intense night together.

From the horror on her face, it's clear she remembers me.

And when the horror fades and her face creases in a dark scowl, I have to wonder if she doesn't have the same happy memories of our night together as I do.

"What are *you* doing here?" she sneers.

"I live here," I say mildly. "Why are *you* here?"

She scowls. "I'm supposed to go on a date with your brother."

My insides turn to ice. "What?"

I don't like the idea of her going out with Al. I don't know her, I don't have any claim on her, we haven't spoken in more than three years, but…

Vivienne scoffs. "Don't worry. I'm canceling."

"Why?"

"I can't do this." She shakes her head. "You need to fuck off."

My eyebrows go up and I cross my arms over my chest. "You're the one who ran into me. I live here."

She rolls her eyes. "Whatever, princess. Get out of my way."

She tries to push past me, and automatically, my hand darts out and grabs her arm.

Before I know what's happening, she shoves me, and then her forearm is pressed against my airway as she gets me in a headlock.

"Don't fucking touch me," she snarls, squeezing my throat.

"Sorry," I croak. I tap her hand, trying to breathe. My vision starts to go black.

Finally, she releases me. Choking back air, I take a step backward, dusting off my jacket.

"Was that really necessary?" I ask in as dry a tone I can manage.

"Fuck off," she says, rolling her eyes.

"We should talk," I suggest. "Grab coffee."

"Why?"

I look her up and down. "I think you know why."

It may have taken three years for our paths to cross again, but that doesn't mean we can't rekindle things where we left off. Just because she never messaged me back doesn't mean my feelings changed.

She shakes her head. "There's nothing to talk about."

"So you remember me."

"The worst mistake of my life?" Viv scoffs. "Yeah, I'd say so."

My heart pounds.

The worst mistake of her life?

She's the highlight of mine.

"Vivienne—"

"Fuck off," she snarls again. "Just—don't. You live your life, I'll live mine, and we'll never have to do this again."

"You're my sister's team captain," I point out.

She scowls. "How did you know that?"

"Are you kidding? Cari can't stop talking about you. She has some serious hero worship going on." I take a step forward. "Look, hate me all you want, but Cari likes you. She looks up to you."

She frowns. "She shouldn't."

"Why not?"

Let me in. Drop your guard, I try to tell her.

She seems to snap back to herself. Her scowl deepens.

"Fuck off," she snarls again. "Just—go away. Leave me alone."

With a sigh, I turn back to the front stoop. I'm ready to get this day over with.

A thought comes to mind, and I turn back to her with a second wind, ready to give her something to think about.

But she's already gone.

Shaking my head, I let myself into the house I share with my siblings. Our parents retired to Miami a few years ago, mainly to take care of my *abuela*. For a while, I rented out rooms to my teammates, but when Carolina graduated from Harvard last spring, she needed a place to stay. And I'm not about to tell my baby sister she can't live in her childhood bedroom. Alberto? Well, he signed a three-year contract with Boston over the offseason. I didn't expect him to stay for more than a few days, but as we wind down preseason and he starts the hockey season in earnest, he's making no attempt to move out.

So I guess I live with my siblings again. At twenty-nine, I would rather not have roommates. I would also rather not work three jobs to pay my way, but hey, I do what I need to do in order to survive.

That's my motto: Do what I need to do.

Inside the house, Cari is sitting in front of the couch, foam rolling her legs.

"Hey," she says as I hang up my coat. "Have you seen Al?"

I look behind me. "No? Isn't he at practice?"

She shrugs. "He was supposed to have a date."

With a hum, I step into the house and make my way to the kitchen. I'm starving.

"There are *frijoles* on the stove," Cari calls as I open the fridge.

"Thanks." I grab the glass container of meal prepped chicken and vegetables, dumping it into a bowl. After a quick turn in the microwave, I add in two scoops of black beans and mix it all together.

With three professional athletes in the house, food is a commodity. All three of us adhere to different dietary standards. Twice a week, one of us will make a few pounds of chicken breast and some vegetables, and then we can doctor it up to meet our individual macronutrient goals. I'll be honest, I'm the best cook out of the three of us, but I also have the least amount of time. Alberto tends to throw things in the slow cooker, Cari likes to experiment with recipes, but for me, cooking is just another chore. It's something I have to do. Especially as an athlete. If I want to eat, if I want to make sure I'm getting the proper nutrients to fuel my workouts, I have to cook.

Doesn't mean I have to like it though.

I eat my meal standing at the kitchen island, scrolling through my phone. I have four hours off before I have to head downtown for my shift at the fancy steakhouse. Do I like serving pretentious twats overpriced steak and seafood? No. Do I depend on the paycheck? Yes.

Do what I need to do.

As I head upstairs, I tug on Cari's ponytail, and she scowls and swats at me. But she's hiding a smile as she does, so I don't think she's really upset.

I've claimed the master bedroom as my own. Al has the room we shared growing up. Cari has her old bedroom. The basement has our home gym. All three of us make use of it.

But as I collapse onto my bed, I can't sleep. My mind is wired.

Vivienne Gallagher.

As long as we lived in Boston, there was always a chance we'd cross paths, but I could leave it up to fate to intervene.

And now it has, I guess.

Because of my sister. Her teammate.

When I thought about what would happen when I saw her again, I didn't expect to freeze. I didn't expect her to hate me. I didn't expect her to go on a date with my brother.

But I froze.

And she hates me.

And for some unknown reason, she likes Al.

Not me. My little brother.

Al is a catch. He's a professional hockey player in the prime of his career. I'm over the hill. I'll probably be forced to retire soon. He makes more money than I do too. He makes more in one season than I'll probably make throughout my entire career. Probably more than twice what I'll earn, let's be real. There aren't a lot of endorsement opportunities for aging male gymnasts who can't bring home medals.

Rolling over, I punch the pillow. I *did* bring home a medal. One medal. A team medal. I'm not dismissing the work our team put in to bring home that bronze. My four events contributed to our team score.

But it's different from winning a medal in my own right. When it came time for my events, I failed. I couldn't close it out.

World Championships are in six weeks. I want to be there. I want to prove my worth.

If I make it to Worlds, I might be able to make another Olympic roster. I can redeem myself.

But first I need to go to work.

four

. . .

Viv

TONY GONZALES. I finally have a name to put to the face.

For the last three years, I've kind of glossed over the fact that my rock bottom happened at the Olympics with another Team USA athlete. I guess it wasn't out of the question to run into them again.

But I didn't expect it to happen *now*.

When I woke up naked and alone... I've never been so low. So used. I was in the prime of my career, celebrating the pinnacle of success at the motherfucking *Olympics*, and instead of celebrating that, I got wasted and hooked up with some dude I barely remembered who couldn't even be bothered to stay for a damn minute once he used me to get his rocks off.

It was sex. A one-night stand. A hookup. There were no feelings involved. It was instant attraction, lubricated by the copious amounts of alcohol we both consumed.

And yeah, for some people, it might not have been a big deal. Even for me, six months prior, it might not have been a big deal.

But that night—and the morning after?

That's a low I've never experienced before. It's something I never want to experience again.

He didn't take advantage of me. I consented. Fuck, I was more than willing.

Something about the way he left me, naked and alone, rubbed me the wrong way. It still does.

It impacted my play in the final match. Yeah, Team USA walked away with a silver medal, but we could have won gold. We could have done better if I didn't have my head in the clouds, trying to process. I'm the reason our team failed. I'm the reason we didn't win.

Maybe that makes me arrogant. As a co-captain, there was a responsibility on my shoulders that I didn't uphold. I didn't play my best, and I didn't have the headspace to encourage my team to be their best, either.

I haven't touched a drop of alcohol since. I don't need it in my life. Maybe it wasn't the alcohol that made me feel that way, but it sure didn't help. I don't go to meetings; I don't need a support group. I just don't want alcohol in my life.

When I reach my apartment, I head upstairs and immediately run a bubble bath. I want to go for a run. I want to scream or yell or punch something. But I can't. That wouldn't serve me.

Sliding into the bath with a protein shake and a good novel helps. I get lost in the book for a bit. My friend Sadie is the author—Sylvie Hirsch is her pen name. She runs a book club and I've met some great friends there… including some with ties to the Boston Grizzlies organization.

See, it's a good thing that Al and I never made it to our date, I tell myself. We have people in common. The sports world is too small. The city is too small.

Shit! I never texted him!

Sloshing in the tub, I pull out my phone and click on his contact. There's a new message from him.

> Cari mentioned you had to go. Sorry for
> running late. Rain check?

Deliberating for a moment, I finally text back:

> I don't think it's a good idea. Your sister is my
> teammate. It could get messy.

Chewing on my lip, I watch the little bubbles dance for a moment as he types.

> Fair enough. I'll catch you around.

A second later, another message.

> If I show up at a Revolution game, it's
> because I'm cheering on my sister. Not trying
> to stalk you.

I laugh.

> Noted. Same if I end up at a Grizzlies game.
> I'm supporting the team.

> Take care, Viv.

With a sigh, I close my phone and sink back into the bubbles. That could have gone a lot worse.

Why couldn't Al be related to literally anyone else in the world? Now that I've seen the two of them in the same photograph, I can see the similarities. I didn't get a chance to know Al. It's all tainted by his brother.

Tony.

Tony Gonzales.

Hey, at least I have a name to put with the face, I rationalize to myself. At least I don't have to think of him as "some random dude" anymore.

Although… maybe that would have been better than knowing he's my teammate's big brother.

———

The animal shelter is a small brick building in the middle of downtown. It is *not* what I was expecting an animal shelter to look like. It's only fall, but there's a chill to the air that permeates the building. And the animals inside? They look so sad, huddled up in tiny balls in their cages. I almost want to reach out and soothe the poor critters.

I'm low-key afraid of animals. It's not something I talk about because who the hell doesn't like animals? When I was three years old, my neighbors' dog got loose and came over and attacked me. Sure, she attacked me with kisses, she was supposedly a sweet thing, but for three-year-old me, it was terrifying to be knocked to the ground, the dog's heavy paws on my chest pinning me down as she slobbered all over me. I couldn't escape. I couldn't get free.

Just because the dog meant no harm doesn't negate the terror I felt. Every time I see a dog, no matter how cute they are, I always expect them to pounce on me and leave me defenseless again.

I never want to feel helpless again.

But when the team PR whiz asked for volunteers for this media appearance, I couldn't say no. As Alycia reminds me, I need to take every opportunity to put myself in the spotlight. Rugby fans know who I am, thanks to my decade-long career, but the public does not. And if I want to keep any endorsement campaigns after I retire next summer, I've got to increase my public presence.

So: animal shelter. Last week, I went to the children's hospital. That might have started out as work, but it turned into fun. Next week, I'm sure there's another appearance on my docket.

Kiana, Andi, Cari, and I are here to help for a few hours. Whatever that means, I'm not sure.

"Welcome, welcome," Susan, the shelter director, says as she ushers us inside. We're followed by Eden, the team's photographer. "We're so glad you're here."

"Thank you for having us. I'm Viv, the team captain," I introduce, shaking her hand firmly. Her grip is limp.

"We're happy to finally meet Carolina's teammates," she chirps.

Cari blushes. "I used to volunteer here," she says awkwardly.

Oh. I clear my throat. "So we're all family here."

Cari giggles nervously. This is her first PR appearance. We'll help her through it.

Susan takes us on a brief tour of the facility. There's a play room for the kitties and a small indoor/outdoor area for the doggies. Staff are cleaning cages, playing with the animals, generally taking care of them.

I have to admit, they do look kind of cute. But then I start to think about petting one, and my heart starts to pound, and I have to take a step back.

A tall man in a black T-shirt is on his hands and knees, coaxing a kitten out of her enclosure. My eyes fall to his backside, taking in the solid muscles. He has a wide, bitable booty and sturdy thighs. As an athlete, I know when people work out. And this guy? He works out. His strong, inked arms flex and his muscles bunch under his T-shirt.

Involuntarily, I let out a soft whimper, biting my lower lip as I salivate over the dude.

Kiana smirks and elbows me. "Are you going to…?"

I shake my head. "Bad idea."

He's staff. He didn't come to work and ask to be sexualized. He didn't come to work to be sexually harassed. I don't like when it happens to me; the least I can do is extend basic courtesy to him too.

I haven't told anyone about my run in with Tony Gonzales the other day. I never told anyone about what happened between us. How could I, when I didn't know his name? And now knowing the worst mistake of my life is my teammate's brother…

Cari pops up like a jack-in-the-box. "What's a bad idea?"

Kiana clears her throat. "Nothing."

She pouts. "Come on. Don't leave me out."

"I was thinking of getting a kitten, but it's a bad idea," I hurry to lie. "I travel too much."

Not to mention their claws terrify me. Sharp little devil blades. My younger sister had a cat growing up and I still have a scar on my chest from when she scratched me.

Cari's face clears. "Oh. I get that. My brothers want to get a pet. I keep talking them out of it."

My scowl at the mention of her brothers is automatic.

She frowns. "Did Al reach out to you? Were you able to reschedule?"

"Yeah, that's not going to happen," I say casually, sticking my hands in my pockets. "It's messy."

"But—"

I shake my head. "What are we doing today?"

Susan details our jobs. There's dog walking, feeding, and cleaning out the cages on offer.

"I'll clean the cages," I immediately announce. Hopefully, they'll be empty.

"Great, Tony will show you what to do," Susan says.

My stomach sinks.

When Cari said she worked here… and now there's a guy named Tony here…

Slowly, I turn around, and sure enough, there is Tony Gonzales, scowling with a tiny black kitten clutched in his massively muscular arms.

"Come on," he grunts, jerking his chin. "We're this way."

Kiana raises her eyebrows, looking between us. I shake my head.

"I don't have all day," Tony snaps.

five

. . .

Tony

I DON'T WANT her here. She's dangerous.

Vivienne Gallagher winds up in *my* animal shelter? This isn't a coincidence. I sense tomfoolery afoot, and I know exactly who to blame.

Glaring at my sister, she smiles innocently at me as I head toward the back room. I've gotten most of the kitten cages taken care of, so only the adult cats need theirs done.

Setting Shadow back in her cage, she gives a pathetic mewl. She has serious separation anxiety. I can't relate, so I stroke the top of her head.

"I'll be back soon," I tell her, and she bats at my hand with her little paws, clinging to me until I gently untangle myself. My icy heart thaws a teeny tiny bit.

And then I glance at Vivienne, wearing a scowl on her face that tells me in no uncertain terms she still hates me, and my insides turn to ice again.

I can't force her to not hate me. But that doesn't mean the cats can't get some much-needed help.

The shelter is chronically under-funded. I'm lucky to get a salary at all. I get paid just above minimum wage for fifteen hours of work a week and usually volunteer another five to ten, depending on my training schedule and my shifts at the restaurant.

The animals need the help. It's not their fault. They deserve better.

Vivienne follows me into the cat room, her face impassive. She crosses her arms over her chest.

"What do you need me to do?" she demands, an edge to her tone and a set to her jaw telling me in no uncertain terms she'd rather be anywhere else.

"We have to clean out the cages, refresh the water bowls, change the litter, and swap out the blankets."

We have an adoption event tomorrow, so the place needs to be clean and tidy, ready for well-meaning visitors who rile up the cats and end up leaving empty-handed. I scowl, thinking about it. The cats don't get their hopes up, but I do. I want them to go to a good home. But the shelter is better than a *bad* home, so maybe they're better off staying here after all.

If I could, I'd adopt every single cat and dog in this shelter. Not only is that not healthy or feasible, it doesn't make sense when they could go to a better home. I'm barely home. I don't have the time to give a dog the attention and exercise it deserves. Besides, I think my siblings may complain if I turn our house into a halfway home for abandoned animals.

No, I'll do better to stick to my current plan: volunteer at the shelter, work my ass off, and hopefully go to vet school soon.

Now I just have to figure out a way to pay for it. Vet school costs *at a minimum* $200,000 for all four years, and that's only if I get into the only in-state program. Most likely, I'd have to go out of state, which increases the cost of tuition, plus the cost of living expenses. I can't rely on an academic scholarship. The only way I got through undergrad on minimal loans was my athletic scholarship, and not only have I used all of my eligibility, there aren't athletic scholarships for most graduate programs.

I've already taken the GRE and the MCAT. My scores are theoretically good enough to get into Tufts here in Boston, but it's an incredibly competitive program. I'd probably have better luck at a different school. Except then I wouldn't be able to live with my siblings and split bills…

Shaking my head, I focus on cleaning out the cages. Vivienne works silently on the opposite side of the room. I'm able to complete three cages to every one she does… but she's doing it. She may be slow about it, a bit skittish when it comes to the chore, but she's not shying away from the hard work.

"I didn't know you would be here," I venture into the silence, punctuated by her movements in the other cages.

She doesn't respond.

"Do you do a lot of these types of things?"

Still nothing. I don't know what I'm looking for. Any sort of reaction. The only thing I don't want is apathy. I don't think I'd be able to handle that.

"Al mentioned you guys were texting," I say casually.

She whirls around. "Are you here to work or to gossip?"

Victorious, I run my tongue over my teeth. "You tell me."

Vivienne scowls. "Fuck off."

"You know, you keep saying that phrase. I don't think you know what it means."

Her face goes red. "You—don't quote *The Princess Bride* at me."

"As you wish." I tip my non-existent hat.

She blusters, her face nearly turning purple. Her eyes bulge and her lips flatten into a firm line. She looks absolutely fucking gorgeous—and absolutely fucking *pissed*.

"Fuck. Off."

Miming zipping my lips shut, I turn around and focus again on my tasks. I feel the heavy weight of her stare on my back for several long moments before she shuffles back to her cages.

We work in silence for a good hour. I shouldn't antagonize her; that will definitely not help my case. Not that I know what I want from her. For her to not hate me, maybe. That would be a good start.

Is it so wrong that I want her to like me? If nothing else, I'd at least like us to be able to speak civilly toward one another. For Cari's sake, if not for mine.

Jennifer, who has the afternoon shift, enters the adult cat room.

"How's it going?" She grabs a clipboard and starts checking I've documented everything.

"Pretty well," I tell her, finishing up the last cage. "They're fairly well-behaved today."

"Good. Just in time for tomorrow." She smirks at me.

We both love and hate adoption fairs. It's good for the animals that find new homes. It's depressing for the ones that don't.

After a few minutes' discussion about what I've done and what still needs doing, Jennifer shoos me away.

Clocking out, I grab my leather jacket and shrug it on before making my way back to Shadow. She's curled into a ball in her cage, but as I approach, she perks up, meowing and dancing in front of the cage door.

Opening it, I scoop her out and tuck her into the front of my jacket, carefully zipping her in. I think I hear what sounds like a sigh and an "aww" from one of the rugby players behind me, but I carefully ignore it. I'm not doing this for her, whoever she is.

I'm doing this for *myself*.

My motorcycle is parked out back. I pull on my helmet and Shadow pokes her head up in the collar of my jacket. When she gets bigger, I can put her in a sidecar, but for now, this is safest for her.

The bike rumbles to a start and she meows excitedly, kneading my chest. I pat her clumsily over the jacket.

With one last look over my shoulder, I see the rugby players staring. My sister is amused, Susan is shaking her head, and if I'm not mistaken, the team's photographer just took a picture of me.

My eyes flick to Vivienne. She's scowling again, her arms crossed over her chest.

Inside my helmet where nobody can see, I smile. She looks so fucking pissed. I love it.

six

. . .

Viv

I NEED A DRINK.

That's my first thought, and the fact that I don't hesitate is enough to give me pause. Alcohol is not the solution to my problems; it's the cause of it.

"Do you have what you need?" I ask Eden, who nods. "First round's on me."

"Thanks, Viv," Andi says, giving me a happy smile. "Top shelf, right?"

I roll my eyes as we head to the pub down the road.

She grins, linking her arm through mine. "So tell me. Was that hottie everything we thought he would be?"

"What hottie?" I ask innocently.

"The guy you couldn't stop salivating over." Kiana fans her face. "When he came out with that kitten, I think my ovaries combusted."

Cari gags. "Gross. That's my brother."

"I was not *salivating*," I tell her evenly. "I was working. As were you."

"Uh huh. *Working*," Eden says, clearly amused. "Is that what you call it, hiding away in the back room all by yourself?"

Fuck. I should have been out front, doing things that were worthy of being photographed. I want to do good deeds for the sake of doing good deeds, yes, but I also need them to be documented. If I want an endorsement campaign, I can't hide away.

"Don't worry, I got the photos I need," Eden continues, holding up her camera.

"Including the dude on his bike?" Andi asks.

Eden smirks. "I think I'm going to start a calendar. Hot guys holding small animals. It'll be a hit."

I scowl. "Don't they have to sign a photo release for that?"

Kiana laughs. "Yeah. *That* is what you're concerned about?" She shakes her head. "We have got to sort out your priorities."

"Oh yeah? Like playing isn't enough of a priority?" I counter.

"We've got to get you laid," Andi announces.

I skitter to a stop. "What?"

"Come on. You were supposed to go on a date with Cari's brother," she continues.

Cari grins. "If Al isn't your type, maybe Tony—"

"*No.*" The word comes out harsh and all four of them stop to stare at me. "It's a bad idea to go out with teammates' family members. Especially as captain. I can't be the cause of drama on the team. No, it's better not to get involved at all."

Kiana rolls her eyes. "Yeah, okay. Whatever."

Truth be told, it *has* been a while for me. The hookup scene is getting old. My friend Rachel just started dating a hockey player on the Grizzlies, and although I'm happy for her, I can't help but feel sorry for myself at the same time.

Nobody is falling head over heels for me. I'm too bitter, too caustic. I'm fun for a night but nobody wants to keep me for longer. I'm secure enough in my body, I know my muscles are what makes me strong and sexy, but the fact remains, a lot of guys are intimidated by women who work out and are stronger than them. It considerably lowers my chances.

I typically date other athletes. When Rach started dating Jake, he introduced me to some of his friends… but nobody struck a spark. It doesn't help that I have a brother who plays hockey in the same league, plus another brother who plays in the NFL. For some reason, they have issues setting me up with their teammates. I can't imagine why.

At the pub, I order a tonic water and lime and take in the room. It's a cozy, run-down kind of vibe. The floor is sticky beneath my sneakers and there's a hazy glare from the yellowed lamps lighting the pub.

Andi settles across the table from me and folds her hands. "Okay, so let's get serious here for a minute," she says. She pins me with a look. "Do you need an intervention?"

My eyebrows go up. "An intervention for what?"

"You haven't gone out with anyone in a while," Kiana points out.

"Maybe she likes being single," Eden cuts in. "She doesn't have to go out with a different guy every weekend."

"Well, no," Andi agrees. "But at least once in a while."

"Know any cute, single guys?" I ask her pointedly. "Preferably someone who won't be emasculated by the fact that I can bench press their weight?"

She sits back in her chair. "Fuck, you think I've been hiding him away? I'm looking for someone too."

Cari tilts her head. "Have you tried any apps?"

I swallow carefully. "You'll want to stay away from apps," I warn her.

"Why? If it's just a hook up…"

Kiana shakes her head. "You're a semi-public figure now. If you're on Tinder and some dude bro screenshots it, you could tank your endorsement opportunities. To the advertising companies, we're supposed to be strong and capable and sexy, but not actually sexually active. And if you're straight, you need to be single, because as soon as you're in a relationship, they lose interest. Lesbians can share the spotlight because it typically furthers their cause and, frankly, we need all the representation of healthy relationships. Straight women are only meant to be some guy's arm candy."

Cari blinks. "Really? They still think that way?"

"Oh, sweetie." I pat her hand. "Just you wait."

It's sick and twisted and disgusting. I'm just one person going up against giant corporations who have more money than sense. I can't change the system.

It's only *part* of the reason I've stayed single. Before the last Olympics, I genuinely was fine dating casually. After, I stopped dating altogether. A few clandestine hookups left me feeling empty. It wasn't like that morning, when I felt like the world was crashing down around me. It just didn't leave me feeling fulfilled.

But fuck, I miss sex. I miss *good* sex. Hot, sweaty, panting for breath, can't get it off my mind sex. It's been forever and a half since I've had that.

It almost makes me wish the date with Al had gone on, but I know it's for the best that we didn't. Dating teammates' siblings is really not a good idea. And on top of that, he plays in the same league as my brother. The last thing I need is this getting back to Chuck and him getting all up in my business. Not to mention the press. *Ugh.* I can only imagine the media shitstorm it would cause if I dated my brother's colleague and my teammate's brother *and then it didn't work.* I'd surely be the biggest media punching bag since... I can't even imagine a similar scandal. Maybe the Russian Olympic doping thing.

No, it's a good thing it's over before it even started. I'm just going to have to meet a guy organically. Like I told Cari, dating apps are out of the question. I can't risk my reputation, my career, for a one-night stand. There are apps for athletes and public figures, but they have to vet you to get you into their system, and somehow, I doubt I'm a big enough name to qualify.

Big enough to have to be mindful about it, but not so much that I'd be on the lists. Outside of the rugby community, nobody knows who I am. All it takes is one good season to knock us into the mainstream media—or one big scandal.

seven

. . .

Tony

THE GYM IS where I go to be myself. The U.S. Gymnastics Men's National Team has a facility in Waltham, and though we don't *have* to train there, strictly speaking, we can train at any gym in the country that accepts us; it's the best facility in the country. Plus, it is practically in my backyard. I'd have to drive farther to go to a lesser quality gym in the suburbs.

There are a handful of major competitions each year, and each member of the national team is gunning for a bid on each assignment. A guy might get one or two major assignments each year. Each competition's score determines eligibility for the big ones like Worlds and the Olympics next summer. There are also smaller competitions, ones that don't result in qualifying the team for major championships and have a decent prize money purse attached to them.

I started gymnastics relatively late. When I was seven, Cari was one and a half, and our parents signed her up for gymnastics. She looked adorable in her little leotard, her diaper sticking out underneath the spandex fabric. Al was in hockey already, but I hated being on the ice, so I'd tag along to the gym.

And I fell in love.

Cari stopped doing gymnastics by the time she was five or six, moving into other sports, but I was already on track for an elite competitive career by then. I made the junior national team at fourteen and competed internationally by seventeen. It helped earn me a full-ride athletic scholarship to Cal Berkeley. I've competed at two different World Championships; I've been to the Olympics. I still want more. I want to *win*.

But I also want to move on to the next stage of my life. My body doesn't rebound the way it used to. The younger guys are getting the more coveted assignments. I can still hold my own on the competition floor, but it takes more and more work to get there.

And I'm *tired*. Outside of training, my job at the steakhouse, and my days at the animal shelter, I don't have any time for *myself*, and when I do, it usually involves cleaning the house and taking care of my siblings. Sure, they're adults. That doesn't mean they're good about cleaning the bathroom or emptying the dishwasher or any of the other things that have to get done.

I'm sure if I asked Al for the money for vet school, he'd give it to me or at least offer me a loan. I don't want to do that. Mixing money and family is tricky business. I've seen enough friendships dissolve over it that I can't do it. As much as I complain about Al, I don't think I'd be able to handle us not speaking. He's my brother. I love him. Even if sometimes I want to strangle him.

Inside the studio, Brody, my old teammate from Cal, is stretching on a yoga mat. He gives me an up-nod as I enter the room and unroll my mat. About half of our workouts are self-guided. Coach Jack and the rest of the training staff will guide us on the actual apparatus. We have a certain number of other workouts we do per week. Strength, conditioning, cardio, stretching... that part is mostly on our own, and we have semi-regular check-ins with Coach to check on our progress.

"What's up, dude?" Brody says as he stretches his hamstring. "I've barely seen you the last few weeks."

"Work stuff," I mutter, starting my stretching routine.

Nobody here knows about my time at the animal shelter or my plans for vet school. They think the steakhouse keeps me busy.

"I feel that," Brody nods, switching sides. He's a personal trainer at a franchised gym and coaches kids' gymnastics at another in the suburbs. "Sometimes I get so tired, I sit on the couch for hours and disassociate."

Grunting my agreement, I pretend like I can relate. I would love a few hours to do nothing.

Shadow, essentially my shadow, has taken most of my free time lately. She's having serious separation anxiety. This morning: This morning, I took her to the shelter for a playdate with the other kittens. I'll pick her back up after training and my shift there, and then she'll come home with me. I'm not ready to leave her alone at the house all day yet. Thirteen hours is a *long* time for a kitten to be on her own, even with treats and toys to keep her occupied.

I wasn't planning on bringing her home. She'd follow me around the shelter whenever possible, complain when I wasn't playing with her, and generally make a nuisance of herself with any of the other staff. Susan thinks she imprinted on me. I don't know if that's really a thing or if she's been reading too many werewolf romance novels again. I just know that the little black kitten makes me happy, and I'll do anything to make sure she's safe and comfortable. If that means bringing her home with me each night, I'll do it. She stole my heart with the first tiny little meow.

After I get stretched and warm, I spend a few hours training under Coach's watchful eye. My new vault combination is freaking fantastic—when I nail it. Half the time, I misjudge the landing and end up on my ass.

That's part of gymnastics *and* part of life. Sometimes you

do some really incredible feats and still end up on your ass. Doesn't mean it's over. You just have to brush yourself off and do it again.

And again.

And again.

Until your muscles are burning and your heart is pounding and you feel like you might die. *That's* when it kicks in. *That's* when you nail it.

And when I stick the landing? It feels fucking phenomenal.

"That was awesome," Brody says, from where he's hanging out on the side of the vault. He's serving as my spotter, ready to intercept if I look like I'm about to crash onto my neck. "You really got it down."

"Now just have to do it again," I mutter, reaching for my water bottle.

He hands it to me as I unwind the wraps around my wrists. "You will. You did it once. You can do it again."

Making a noise of agreement, I gulp down my water. I'm drenched with sweat, my muscles sore from a good day's work.

After a quick break, I get back to work. I'm pleased when I land more than half of the vaults. The combination is new for me. I can do a round-off and back handspring into three and a half twists laid out on the floor. No problem. It's when I do it off the vault that I struggle.

But if it was easy, everyone would do it. And there's a reason only a handful of guys in the world are able to throw the Shirai II vault. I'm one of them. Sometimes.

I get the theory of it. I understand where I'm going wrong. That doesn't mean fixing it is any easier.

When Coach claps his hands and declares my time is up, I'm so relieved, I collapse on the mat.

"Go cool down," he barks.

Brody steps toward me with my water again.

"Don't you have to practice?" I snipe as I snatch the bottle from his hand.

He laughs. "You're grouchy today."

"Shut up," I mutter.

He shoves me gently. "Come on. I've got to do some time on the high bar. You can spot me."

Grumbling under my breath, I follow him across the gym. There are plenty of other people around that could spot him.

Lifting him to the high bar, he does a few swings around the bar before he hangs there, stretching his arms and shoulders.

"A few guys were talking about going out to the bar after this," Brody says, folding into a pike and then stretching into the laid out position. He does a series of toe-touches, alternating between pike and straddle.

Letting out a sigh, I sink onto the mat and stretch. My legs are so sore, they're almost shaking.

"You need to come," he continues.

I roll my eyes. "Pass."

"Come on," he wheedles. "You never come out with us."

"Yeah, because I'm—" I cut myself off abruptly.

"You're what?" Brody asks.

"I'm not up for socializing right now," I finally say.

"You just need to get laid," he says.

I make a face. I don't like to talk about my personal life. It's personal for a reason.

"Come on. You could use a break. You're always working or training. When do you ever take time for yourself?"

I open my mouth.

"That's right, never," Brody pushes. "You're going to burn out, man. Then you'll crash and get hurt right before Worlds. We need you on that team. We can't bring home a medal without you."

"I don't have the time," I say honestly. "I have to work."

"Do you work today?" he demands.

"Well—no."

"So tonight, you're coming out with us," he says, as if he's decided for me. "It's been forever since the guys got together. Frankly, we could all use a night out."

With a groan, I hang my head. "Why are you so obsessed with me?"

Brody laughs, swinging around the bar in a simple giant. "So that's a yes?"

This is *not* what I wanted to spend my evening doing. I was looking forward to a nice evening off, not going anywhere or seeing anyone or doing anything.

But I also know he won't rest until I give in.

"Ugh. Fine."

eight

. . .

Viv

A YEAR AGO, I'd never have thought I'd be up close and personal with the Boston Grizzlies schedule. Sure, Vanessa is dating Sven and works for the team. But then Sadie's new boyfriend joined the team staff too. And now Rachel started dating their goalie.

Tonight is an away game and the girls are gathering to watch the game at Ceci's insistence. I'm not sure why she's so invested in getting all of our book club to watch the games. They have over eighty games in a season. I'm not associated with the team, plus my brother plays for *another* team. I have no reason to watch the Grizzlies.

When Ceci declared we were gathering, I knew I couldn't get out of it. Not without lying outright, and I don't lie to my friends. *I don't feel like it* is not a good enough reason for Ceci. As much as I love her, she's *a lot*. She knows it, and she listens and backs off when we tell her we need space. Usually.

It's been a week since I ran into Tony at the animal shelter, and I've only thought about it, like, seventeen times a day since. The sight of all those tattooed muscles wrapped up in a leather jacket, holding a tiny little kitten on his motorcycle...

My pulse throbs at the memory and I lick my lips automatically.

"Okay, seriously," Sadie says, cutting into my thoughts. "What's up with you?"

"Nothing. What's up with you?" I turn the tables on her.

"You're distracted," she says, eyeing me curiously. "I know watching the Grizzlies isn't your favorite thing to do, but—"

"I support all Boston sports." It's kind of my job.

She shakes her head. "That's not what I mean."

"How's Chuck?" Ceci cuts in. I wasn't even aware she was paying attention to us.

"He's fine." I think. Actually, I haven't talked to my brother in a bit. I'm not even sure if he's home or away right now.

"Send him my love," Ceci says, waggling her eyebrows.

She has a weird fascination with my brothers and flirts with both of them whenever they're in town. Perry and Chuck are twins but have completely different career paths. Chuck is a forward for the Colorado hockey team and Perry is a defensive back for the Raleigh football team. It depends on the day which one she's more interested in.

Neither of them has any interest in her, but in the three years I've known her, she hasn't been deterred. I don't think she'd actually *pursue* them. It's more the idea of needling me. She's the world's biggest flirt with absolutely zero follow-through.

Laughing, I thaw out a bit. "I'll be sure to do that."

Sipping my soda, I take in the bar. Despite being in Cambridge, it's not a college student bar. Thank goodness. I'm a little too old to be hanging out in the same type of grungy dive bars of my youth. I'm on the younger side of my friend group, Ceci on the older end.

The chime above the door rings out, and I glance in that

direction automatically. My drink goes down the wrong pipe and I choke.

"What's wrong?" Rachel asks.

My eyes are glued to the group of men standing in the doorway, led by Tony fucking Gonzales in his motherfucking leather jacket.

Is he aware that a hot tattooed man on a motorcycle in a leather jacket is my weakness?

"Ooh, who's that?" Sadie cuts in, following my gaze. "He is *pretty*."

I scowl at her.

"What? He's pretty. If I wasn't happy with my own man, I'd be all over that hunk like brie on bread."

Shaking my head, I take a deep breath and then take a sip of my soda.

"Do you know him?" Vanessa cuts in.

Wincing, I admit: "He's my teammate's brother."

Ceci cackles so loudly, heads turn in our direction.

Including his.

Tony's eyes go wide and a slow smirk spreads over his face. It shouldn't make him look even more attractive, but unfortunately for me, it does. My stomach flutters and my core throbs.

"Great. I just want to die now," I snap, running my hand through my hair. It's one of the rare occasions it's not tied up in a ponytail or messy bun. For once, I'm not wearing leggings, either; I put on real pants and a real bra to come to this meetup.

"Do we like him?" Sadie asks. "Or do we hate him?"

"Hate," I mutter. The weight of his powerful gaze is still on me. I can't get away from it. My spine itches under his scrutiny.

"Why do we hate your teammate's brother?" Van asks.

With a sigh, I scrub my hands over my face. "Because I

met him first. Three years ago." When they don't react, I whisper. "Biblically."

"Damn, girl," Ceci says. She lifts her hand for a high five. "He looks like the kind to give it to you good."

I'm already in hell. So why not tell them the truth?

They're all aware I'm sober, that it's from an awful experience I haven't wanted to talk about. I'm sure they'll support me unconditionally and they won't spread my secrets.

So why is my stomach churning? I break out into a sweat and have to take a few more deep breaths.

"That night was the last time I drank alcohol. Haven't touched a drop since."

"Shit, girl," Sadie says, shaking her head. She reaches out and squeezes my hand. "Do you want to talk about it?"

"Not really."

"Did he…" Rachel pauses. "Was it all consensual?"

Wincing, I nod. "Yeah. He didn't drug me or anything. I was into it, from what I remember. I just… didn't like the way I woke up. Or how I felt when I did."

"That's perfectly understandable," Van says. She reaches across and takes my hand. "Thank you for sharing with us. It means a lot. We don't take it lightly."

Tears spring to my eyes. It's so sudden and out of character, I don't know what to do.

Rachel gets out of her chair and walks around the table, wrapping me in a hug. "Oh, babe."

"I'm fine. It's fine," I mutter, wiping at my eyes.

"It's okay to not be okay," Sadie says seriously. "That was a big thing to share. A big thing to keep buried deep."

"I'm over it," I lie. I'm definitely not. I thought I was, I'd buried it down deep enough but seeing him again has only proven that I've never actually dealt with it.

"We need food," Ceci declares. "If we're going to spy on this super hot guy we hate, we need snacks."

Forcing a laugh, I wipe away the last remnants of my

tears. "I'll get it. One of everything, right?" That's our usual M.O. when we get together.

Ceci tries to hand over her card, but I wave it away. I don't have her kind of money, but I can treat my friends to bar snacks.

On shaky legs, I make my way to the bar and squeeze into an empty spot. Even though I don't need it, I pick up a menu and pretend like I'm not hiding out.

Why is he here? Of all the bars in the city, he picks the one where I am. If I didn't know better, I'd say he has a tracking beacon installed in my shoe. Except, one, when would he have been able to do that, and two, why would he even care?

We're nothing to each other. It was one night, three years ago. It meant nothing.

Except it changed everything for me.

A warm body slides in beside me. The familiar scent of sandalwood and leather wash over me as Tony fucking Gonzales stands next to me. Why does he have to smell so good? I want to bury my face in his neck and inhale. Except not *his* neck. Just the neck of the guy that smells that good.

He's discarded his leather jacket, resting his forearms on the bar beside me. He doesn't look at me.

"What are you doing here?" I bite out.

To my surprise, he chuckles. "It's always *what are you doing here* with you, never, *hi, it's nice to see you again.*"

"I'm not a liar."

"No, I don't suppose you are," Tony says lightly. "I didn't know you'd be here."

"I'm with my friends." The words are hard to say.

"So am I."

The bartender makes his way over to us, greeting Tony first.

"She was here first," he says, hooking his thumb in my direction.

"What can I get you?" the bartender asks, looking bored.

"One of each on the appetizer menu, plus an extra order of the spicy cauliflower," I order. "Thanks."

He nods at me, walking over to the terminal to enter the order.

"That's a lot of food," Tony comments.

"That's a lot of *none of your fucking business*," I tell him blandly.

The bartender returns with the check. Glancing at the receipt to make sure it's correct, I give him my card.

"What can I get you?" the bartender asks Tony.

Like it's coming through static, I hear him placing an order for multiple drinks. I take a slow, deep breath, but it doesn't help the static feeling inside my head. He makes me lose all sense of myself. I don't like it. I know who I am; I *like* who I am.

I don't like what he's turned me into—now, or back then.

Turning away, I head back to my table. I've only made it two steps when I stumble.

But before I can hit the ground, there are hands catching me. Tony yanks me upright and doesn't let go of me until I'm back on my two feet.

"Careful, there," he says, and I can't decide if I'm reading into it or if he's mocking me. "Damn, how much have you had to drink?"

"I'm sober." I scowl at him. Straightening my shirt, I glare at him. Why did he have to be the one to catch me? "Thanks," I mutter after a beat.

"Anytime," he says, his voice dipping. He leans closer. "Listen—"

I shake my head. I don't want to listen. I don't want to prolong this any longer than I have to.

"I've got to go," I say, hooking a thumb back at my friends.

"Do you want to—"

"No." I want nothing to do with him.

Tony searches my eyes for a moment before he sighs and takes a step back. "Have a good night, Vivienne."

My bad mood sours further. "My name is Viv."

nine

. . .

Tony

"WHO'S THE CHICK?" Brody asks as I pass him his beer.

"Who?" I echo, handing out drinks to the rest of the guys. Dylan is twenty-four and a powerhouse on the rings. Tommy is maybe twenty-six and specializes in parallel bars and the pommel horse. They've both been on the national team since college and Tommy was on last year's Worlds team with me.

"The super hot chick you were chatting up," Dylan says, nodding toward Vivienne's table.

My cheeks heat. "She knows my sister."

Brody's eyebrows go up. "And she looks like she hates you because…?"

I wince. "Because she does."

"Her friends keep looking over here," Tommy comments, shamelessly looking back at them over his shoulder.

"Can you stop being so fucking obvious?" I hiss at him.

"What, do you like her or something?" Brody teases.

Or something.

"She shot me down," I mutter.

Brody laughs. Loudly.

Fucker.

"Come on, man," he says, slinging an arm across my

shoulders. "We'll get you nice and drunk and find you another one to go home with."

"We have training tomorrow morning," I remind him.

He waves it off. "Come on. One night won't kill you."

"She might though," Dylan taunts. "That chick looks like she wants to cut off your dick and feed it to you."

Brody and Tommy wince.

I glance over in Vivienne's direction. Her table is in the direct path of ours, so our eyes meet, and she glares at me so furiously I think a fire might have started. Unable to help myself, I smile and wave my fingers at her. Steam practically rises from her ears, and she turns in her seat so she can't see me.

Damn it. I pushed too hard.

"Yeah," I agree glumly. "But it would be fun."

"You're sick, man," Tommy says, shaking his head.

"Definitely." I take a drink of my beer.

"The heart wants what the heart wants," Brody says sagely.

My eyebrows go up. "Who said anything about my heart?"

He laughs. "In all the years I've known you, I've never seen you this sprung on a woman before. You want more than just a night with her."

Shrugging my shoulders, I try not to crawl into a hole and die. "I mean, have you seen her?"

She's basically every fantasy come to life. Tall, nearly as tall as me, with wide shoulders and strong thighs that felt incredible wrapped around my waist. She's got curves to go with her muscles. Her body is amazing. Her as a person? I like her. I want to know more.

We don't talk about feelings, me and the guys. We have a very surface level relationship. I've met Brody's girlfriend, she came to championships last year, but I never hang out with Tommy or Dylan outside of the gym.

"So it's just physical, then," Tommy says slowly.

"Yeah," I lie. "Just physical."

Vivienne means something to me. Our night together, the night before I brought home the bronze medal at the Olympics, it meant something. We had a connection.

After my events were over, I looked for her, but she was in the semi-finals for her medal, so I kept to myself. I promised myself I would approach her at the Closing Ceremony, but I never got the chance. Too many people were there. She was never alone.

I sent her a few messages on Instagram. She never answered. I'm guessing she was inundated with messages following the Games; I know I was, and I have nowhere near her star power. I didn't have a way to contact her directly. What, was I supposed to call up the national rugby federation and ask for her contact info? She would have thought I was the world's biggest stalker.

Looking back... I do regret the way I left things though. Sneaking out after she fell asleep was a dick move. I can see that now in a way I couldn't have in the heat of the moment three years ago.

Chancing a glance in her direction again, she's talking to her friends, absently twirling a lock of hair around her finger. I never took her as a hair twirling type. I'm filled with the sudden desire to find out what else I don't know about her.

Brody chugs the rest of his beer. "Oh, look, my glass is empty," he says loudly. "I need another. You?"

It's been two point seven seconds since I gave him his drink. I glare at him. "What are you doing?"

He kicks back his barstool and ambles over to the bar. In short order, he's served another beer, plus a short glass of a clear liquid with a lime wedge.

Brody doesn't make his way back to our table though. He cuts his way through the crowd to Vivienne's table.

Shit.

Hopping off my stool, I rush over to intercept him as he's offering the short glass toward her.

"Thanks, but no thanks," Vivienne is saying.

"Come on, it's just a drink," Brody wheedles. "He—" He looks up at me. "What are you doing?"

"Stopping you before you end up wearing that drink," I snap. Turning to her, I offer a chagrined smile. "Sorry about him. He has no sense of self-preservation."

"Nor do you," Vivienne counters with a smirk.

Brody tries to push the drink toward her again.

"Dude, no woman is going to take a drink from a man she doesn't know," I point out. "That's basic safety 101."

Surprise flutters over Viv's face. I wonder why she's surprised.

"Besides, I'm sober," she says again.

"We can fix that," Brody says with a grin.

She shakes her head. "No, I'm sober. As in, I don't drink."

It's my turn to be surprised. The night we met, she was drinking rum and Cokes. I still remember the hint of spice on her breath when I kissed her in the elevator, the way she clung to me as the metal cage rose to the twelfth floor where she was staying.

I remember that night far too well for a random hookup three and a half years ago. I guess that's because she's not just a random hookup to me.

She's my gold medal. Sure, I may have only brought home a physical bronze medal. But that night with her? It meant everything.

Vivienne's friend tosses an arm over her shoulder and leans into her. "Do you guys want to hang out?"

The friend is pretty, with reddish-brown hair falling in curls down her back. She's older than Vivienne, maybe mid-forties.

"I'm Ceci." She introduces herself, then her friends. "This is Sadie, Vanessa, and Rachel."

"Nah, we're here with friends," I answer when Brody doesn't.

He glares at me. I stare back. I'm not a mind reader, so I don't know what he's trying to tell me.

"Bring your friends over," Sadie says. She has wavy brown hair to her shoulders and a simple silver hoop through her nose. "Any friend of Viv's is a friend of ours."

"He's not my friend," Vivienne mutters, glowering at me. "I don't even know him."

And even though I try to laugh it off, I can't deny the words hurt. "She's my sister's team captain," I explain to the friends and Brody.

But from the assessing looks her friends give me, they already know that. I wonder what else she's told them.

"We're gymnasts," Brody says, gesturing between us.

Ceci obviously checks us out. "I'll say," she says, a satisfied smirk turning up her wine-red lips.

My stomach turns. I don't enjoy feeling like a piece of meat. Her sizzle of interest isn't real; it feels like she's forcing it, putting on a show.

A cheer goes up in the bar, and heads swivel toward the nearest TV. The Grizzlies game is on. I should probably follow the game to see how Al's doing.

"Sven scored," the blonde named Vanessa says with a happy smile. She does a little dance in her seat.

"*Someone's* getting laid," Ceci teases.

Vanessa shakes her head. "They're playing in Buffalo. *Someone* is getting home at two o'clock in the morning. We'll celebrate when he wakes up."

It takes me a second to connect the dots. "Are you talking about Sven Larsson?"

Vanessa's smile brightens. "Yeah. He's my boyfriend."

"My brother is on the team too. Alberto Gonzales."

Normally, I don't like admitting my connection to the team. I don't want people to think I'm boasting. Nor do I want the attention that comes along with having a famous sibling. Outside of the gymnastics world, nobody knows who I am—and I like it that way.

"Oh, I love Gonzo," Rachel chimes in. "My boyfriend Jake is the goaltender."

My stomach turns. No wonder Vivienne wanted to date Al. All of her friends are dating players on the team.

"What about you?" Brody asks, pointing the neck of his beer toward Sadie. "You got a boyfriend?"

She laughs. "Yeah. He's an analyst on the intermission show."

Brody's attention turns to Ceci, lifting his eyebrows. I don't know why he's so invested in Vivienne's friends' relationships.

"I'm just a fan," she says with a lascivious grin. "I might have to become a gymnastics fan too."

"It's a great sport," Brody says casually. "I do personal training at a gym in Newton, if you're ever interested in some one-on-one training."

Rolling my eyes, I rap my knuckles twice on the table. "I'm going to head out," I announce. "You don't need me here."

"You sure, man?" Brody asks.

"Yeah. I'm good."

"I guess I better scoot," he says to the women. "It was nice meeting you."

"You too," Vanessa echoes with a warm smile.

Vivienne scowls.

"Why don't you walk your friend out?" Ceci says pointedly.

"He's not my friend," she says.

"But you know him."

"He's barely an acquaintance." Vivienne shakes her head. "He's just another in a long list of mistakes."

ten

· · ·

Viv

HALFWAY THROUGH MY TEN-MILE RUN, the sun has just started peeking out through the clouds, sunbeams lighting the dark gray sky. It's been raining the past few days, the ground slick beneath my feet. My breath comes in soft pants as I try to regulate my breathing.

Kiana, running beside me, has barely broken a sweat. Me? I'm covered in sweat from head to toe. I don't mind it when I'm on the rugby pitch or lifting weights in the gym, but other than that, it is not my favorite sensation.

"Are you going to talk about it?" Kiana asks.

"Talk about what?"

"Whatever has your brain so twisted." She slows to a stop and turns to stare at me, her hands on her hips.

I stop also. "I'm not twisted."

"You've been off for a few days," she points out. "Your game hasn't been on point, either."

I've been playing particularly badly in practice. It's like I've entirely forgotten how to rugby. I'm missing tackles, fumbling passes, and generally being a hindrance on the pitch.

"I've been… distracted," I admit with a wince.

She looks at me, waiting. "Yeah. By what?"

When I don't answer immediately, she pokes me in the shoulder.

"Come on, you used to tell me everything. Does it have anything to do with that super hot guy from the shelter?"

"No." The word comes out hushed and harsh.

A slow smile spreads over Kiana's face. "It does! That's why you've been so weird!"

Grumbling, I stub the toe of my shoe into the ground. "I ran into him last night."

Her eyebrows go up. "And?"

"And nothing. I was with some friends, so was he. His friend was totally obnoxious."

"Are you seriously that freaked out he's Cari's brother?"

Not really. Do I love that he's related to my teammate? No. Would it be enough to stop me from pursuing him? No.

Except that he's…

With a grunt of frustration, I take out my ponytail and tie it up again.

"You're stalling," Kiana accuses.

I could give her excuses, but they'd be just that—excuses.

He brings up bad memories. He makes me insecure. I don't like the way I feel around him.

But I don't want to share any of that. I've already told too many people. Sooner or later, it's going to get back to him, and I am *not* looking forward to that conversation.

"He's not interested in me," I tell her. "So it's a moot point."

"But if he were…"

I shake my head. "He's not. So it doesn't matter."

He's gorgeous, I'll give him that. And we definitely had a spark three years ago.

That doesn't mean I want more. I don't even know *what* I want.

"I'm not really looking to date anyone right now," I finally say.

Kiana laughs. "Who said anything about dating? Screw him and move on."

"Tried that," I mutter. "Didn't work."

Her eyebrows go up. "Excuse me?"

Shit. I didn't mean to say that.

"You can't tell Cari," I tell her urgently.

"I won't." She crosses an X over her heart. "Tell. Me. Everything."

"We hooked up at the Olympics. It was a one and done thing." My cheeks warm, remembering the heat of that night. "I hadn't seen him again until…"

Kiana's mouth drops open. "Was it that bad?"

"Worse." *It was that good.* "So yeah, I'm not looking to go down memory lane. And I'm definitely not trying to start something there. It's just that every time I turn around, there he is."

"Oh, hey," she says, waving exuberantly to someone behind me.

Fuck.

Is he here? Did she see him? Did he *hear*?

I duck my head, trying to hide.

Kiana laughs. "Stop it, you goober. He's not here."

"You're mean." I swat at her shoulder. "That's cruel."

"We just have to find you someone else," she says, like it's that easy.

"I'm not looking for anything…"

"That's when you find it," she says. "When you try to find it, you never will. If you let it happen naturally, it will come to you."

Maybe that philosophy works for dating, but it doesn't apply to the rest of my life. I'm used to pushing, working for what I want. College athletics scholarship? Earned. Make the national team? Named to the team. Go to the Olympics? Done and done. Bring home a medal? Check. Become the best at my sport? Still a work in progress, but I'm still working on it.

So when I get home, before I let myself shower and change, I call my agent. Alycia answers on the second ring.

"I was just about to call you," she says, and I laugh, because that's what she always says.

"Sure. What about?"

"A brand wants to do a few collabs with you."

I sit up straight. "Really?"

"Yeah. They sell some sort of probiotic juice."

Oh.

"Quasi-health food?"

She can probably hear the disappointment in my voice. I like to support products I believe in. I'm not interested in selling myself to the highest bidder; I want there to be substance to the campaigns I promote.

"You don't have to talk about the health benefits. Just how good it tastes and that it's a probiotic," Alycia assures me.

"Does it actually taste good?"

"It's… not bad," she hedges. "The ginger peach flavor is decent."

My laugh is bitter. "So I'd be endorsing a shit product and lying about it to the world."

"Well, when you put it that way…" Alycia sighs. "If you only want campaigns that you fully believe in, you're limiting your options."

"I don't want to lie."

"I don't think of it as lying. It's just…"

"It's lying and deceiving the people who follow me if I don't actually believe in the product. That's a hard limit for me, Alycia," I tell her.

She sighs again. "Okay. I'll tell them no. We can go back to the drawing board."

"Thanks." My voice comes out wooden. I know she's working hard. I know I'm not making it easy on her. "Send me a sample of the juice. I'll try it. Maybe it isn't as bad as you say."

"You got it." I can hear the smile in her voice. "Aside from that, I'm still putting out feelers. Pump It Up Protein wants to do another project with you, but they're still working on concrete plans. They definitely want you."

"I'm in." Pump It Up is one of my regular sponsors. And as a bonus, I actually like their protein powder. They make a watermelon lemonade flavored protein powder that I add to water and sip all day long. "I'm running low on stock."

"I'll see if they can send some more over," Alycia says. "Birdie Sportswear is hosting a dinner next week with some other influencers. Are you interested?"

I've heard of Birdie. They typically feature more petite body types than mine. Lean, slim, toned, their models are usually half my size. There's nothing wrong with that. I just don't fit their usual demographic.

"Are you sure they want *me*?"

I'm not trying to be a Negative Nancy, shutting down all of her suggestions. At the end of the day, I'd rather focus on the real world than on maybes and what ifs. I don't trust that these big brands actually want me to promote their companies. There must be some trickery afoot.

"They're expanding with a new Fit and Strong line," she says. "They reached out first."

In that case…

"Sure, I'll be there."

Alycia and I chat for a few more minutes, debriefing on practice and all the other things in my life. Her firm represents both Chuck and Perry as well as my sister Janine, the champion swimmer, though we all have different agents to prevent conflict of interest. She dated Perry for a hot minute in college before they decided they worked better as friends, and I swooped in and stole her for myself. I've known her for the better part of a decade. She knows my whole family, my history, the reason I'm sober. And never, not once, has she told me to get over it.

Maybe it's a little silly to be holding onto all those strong emotions after all these years. I'm a different person now than I was three years ago. He can't help being the person who brings them all out. If he hadn't left before I woke up, would I still have all this animosity toward him? I honestly don't know.

One thing's for certain; if the last few weeks have taught me anything, it's that no matter where I go, I can't escape him. Between his sister being on my team, his brother being teammates with all my friends' boyfriends, and both of us being professional athletes, we're surely going to keep running into each other, whether we like it or not.

eleven

. . .

Tony

"THIS IS DUMB," I tell Brody, who grins at me.

"You're dumb," he taunts.

Flipping him off, I focus my attention on the field again. Ostensibly, we're here to see Cari. In reality—and the reason Brody tagged along with me—we're here to see Vivienne.

Viv.

I can't call her that. It's an invitation to intimacy that I haven't earned. In my head, she's always going to be Vivienne to me.

On the pitch in front of us, the Boston Revolution are in the middle of a scrimmage, half the team in blood-red jerseys, the rest kitted out in royal blue. Vivienne is the hooker, which means she's responsible for getting the ball backward to her team in a scrum. Cari is the tighthead prop, who helps support her while she's fighting for the ball.

I'll be honest; my sister has played rugby for six years, and no matter how many times she's patiently explained it, I still don't really get the rules of the game. While it's fun to watch, and it's clear they enjoy playing it, I'm not all that interested in contact sports.

In college, despite having a nationally ranked football team, I only went to two games in all four years. Once, my freshman year, was to see what the fuss was about. The second time, they recognized our gymnastics team in front of sixty thousand people for winning the conference championship the year before.

Our meets were lucky if we had six *hundred* spectators.

My social circle in college revolved around gymnastics. If I had a social circle nowadays, it still would. But where men's careers typically take off *after* college, women's careers tend to die down. The disciplines require different levels of strength and flexibility between the sexes. While there are still women competing until their mid- to late-twenties now, there aren't many. Most women training at the national team training center are *young*, like, still in high school, young. I can't hang out with them outside of practice without feeling like a creeper.

Brody and I are the oldest guys on the national team. Everyone else is younger. My friends have all moved on. The guys I went to college with gave up gymnastics and found new callings in life. A few of them became bodybuilders or powerlifters and do competitions. Some are "influencers" promoting themselves on social media. And then the rest have settled into their lives, finding jobs and careers and life trajectories.

I'm stuck in limbo. As much as I want to keep doing gymnastics, my body doesn't. I want to move on to the next stage of my life, I want to go to vet school, but when I think about four more years of school, plus all the debt that will come with it…

I shiver, and Brody raises his eyebrows at me.

"You good, man?" There's actual concern in his voice.

"'M fine," I mutter, zipping up my leather jacket like the brisk wind is the culprit.

We sit in quiet silence for a few minutes, the grunts and noise on the pitch our soundtrack.

"So..." Brody says.

"No."

"Come on. You're not even going to try?"

When he suggested coming to watch the practice, to see Vivienne, I balked. I don't want to do this. I especially don't want to do this in front of a crowd.

But when he threatened to set me up on as many blind dates as it takes to find someone I can jibe with... I asked Cari for two guest passes.

The coach's whistle blows, and the group on the pitch dissembles, grabbing water and electrolytes.

My sister bounds up to us, relaxed and perky despite sweating and working on the field for the last hour and a half.

"You came!" Cari gives me a brilliant smile. "I didn't think you'd actually show up. This is your first time at practice since I signed with the team."

My stomach churns. I haven't been supporting my little sister, not in the way I should be. She thinks I'm here for her when I'm really trying to score some points with her teammate.

"You're looking good out there," I deflect.

"It's all Viv. She's amazing," she says.

My smile falls. What am I doing? Vivienne is my sister's *captain*. They work together every single day. No way can I ask her out, not when it'll make Cari's life infinitely more complicated when this all goes to shit.

A group of women start in our direction, Vivienne hanging in the back.

"You're the motorcycle guy," says a tall, wide woman with cornrow braids tied up in a ponytail. I recognize her from the day the rugby players came to the shelter. "I'm Kiana. This is Andi and Grace," she says, pointing to the other two women. "And you know Viv already."

Vivienne's face, red from exertion, turns nearly purple. "Ki, shut it."

She's sweaty, her hair slick with it and her uniform drenched, but she's never looked more gorgeous to me. Sure, I liked looking at her dressed in casual clothes the other night, her hair and makeup done. Now, natural and in her element? I've never been more attracted to her in my life.

And that's the problem. She makes me stupid. Usually with women, I'm calm, cool, collected. Maybe a little detached. I don't invest emotionally.

But with her… I want to. I don't know what it is about Vivienne that makes me want to break all my rules. It's more than our night together and my winning the next day. It's more than this attraction that thrums in my veins and calls her to me. It's *more*.

"What are you up to later?" Brody asks Cari.

She laughs, flicking her ponytail over her shoulder. "Why? You dump your girlfriend yet?"

His face goes red.

The women are all interested in him, watching with glee. Vivienne is standing a little off to the side, her arms across her chest. As I approach, her stance tenses.

"What are you doing here?" she demands. For once, she's not glaring at me.

"We came to see my sister," I answer lightly.

She rolls her eyes. "Really? The season doesn't start for four more months."

I crack my neck. Here goes.

"Okay. *He* is here to see her. I'm here for *you*."

"Why?"

"I wanted to see you." I try to keep my tone light and breezy, but from the way she frowns and her forehead furrows, I don't think I'm successful.

"Why?" she asks again.

"I wanted to." My stomach swirls with anxiety and my

palms sweat. She isn't making this easy on me. "What are you up to later?"

Vivienne cocks her head. "What do you mean?"

"I mean, what are you up to later?" Do I need to spell it out for her? "Would you like to grab coffee?"

"That's not a good idea," she says, talking a slow stutter-step back.

"Just coffee. Don't read into it."

She shakes her head. "Yeah. Still not a good idea."

"Because…" I cock an eyebrow.

"Because we shouldn't."

"Is a reason that you don't want to?"

She chews her lip. "No?"

"Then I don't see a reason two single, consenting adults can't have coffee together."

Glaring daggers at me, she says, "you know it's more than that."

"It doesn't have to be."

But Vivienne shakes her head. "I—I can't."

My stomach drops. "Okay, then."

I try to pretend like I'm not disappointed. Now that I've finally psyched myself into asking, I have to admit I was looking forward to spending more time with her.

Her mouth opens, but no words come out.

"See you around." Heading over to where Brody and Cari are still flirting, her teammates having walked away, I give him a subtle shake of my head, and he frowns.

"We're going to head out," he announces, jerking his thumb over his shoulder. "You have time to come with us?"

Cari shakes her head. "We've got weights this afternoon. Another time, maybe."

"Yeah, maybe," I echo dumbly.

My sister turns her attention to me, and I shrink under her heavy stare. She's always had a way of knowing exactly what's wrong. I can't tell her about this though. Not about Vivienne.

A beat passes before Cari sighs and shakes her head again.

"I'll catch you at home," she finally says. "Don't do anything dumb."

Does she know me? Dumb is practically my middle name.

twelve

. . .

Viv

"OKAY, I'm going to tell you something, and it's kind of a secret," I tell Cari.

Her eyes go wide and she nods like a bobblehead. "I'll take it to the grave."

I laugh at her earnestness. "It's not that big of a secret. I don't want it spread around the team. It's just… your brother Al…"

"Please tell me you're dating him," Cari blurts.

Maybe doing this on our way to his hockey game was a bad idea.

I wince. "No. But, um… my friends are all dating his friends."

She blinks at me. "What?"

"Two of my good friends are dating players on the Grizzlies," I explain. "And another's boyfriend is the team's reporter. So…"

"So you and Al are perfect for each other, then!" she chirps. "You already have overlapping friend groups!"

I shake my head. "That's why it won't work. It's too incestuous."

Not to mention her *other* brother…

"So why are you telling me?" Cari asks. "Is it that big a deal that your friends are dating Al's teammates?"

"It's not, not really. It's more… I didn't want you to be blindsided if they mention it," I explain. "The wives and partners aren't always super welcoming to me. I'm not officially associated with the team. I think they think I'm after their guys, which I would never do, but they don't know me. We don't sit in the team box with them, so if that's what you were expecting…"

She shakes her head. "Anywhere is fine. I'm just glad you're inviting me along."

Seeing Tony at practice the other day, on top of the night at the bar, drove home the reminder that our lives are inexplicably intertwined. His brother is the teammate of all my friends' boyfriends. His sister is *my* teammate. I can't get away from him.

I don't even know if I want to at this point.

I can't figure out if he was asking me out the other day. I mean, I *think* he was, but I'm not sure the motivation behind it. He acts like he can't stand me, but then he shows up at my practice in his fucking leather jacket with his hair all windswept… and I didn't hate it. Not in the slightest.

Where that leaves me now, I'm not sure.

Ceci couldn't make it tonight, so we're not in a suite. Vanessa's arranged for us to sit on ice level on the Grizzlies shoot twice side. Sadie and Rachel are joining us, of course, plus Hailey MacGregor, the younger sister of Aidan MacGregor. We've met a few times and she seems lovely.

Although Hailey's a few years older than Cari, I thought it might be nice for her to have another sibling-of-a-player there. When I go to Chuck's hockey games and Perry's football games, hanging out with the other wives and partners gets awkward, fast. They view the guys in a very different lens than I see my brothers. I still see them as the annoying little chuckleheads I grew up with. It's easy to forget they're playboy professional athletes who fuck everything that moves.

I'm a professional athlete too, but if I were to fuck any guy who looked at me, I'd be called a slut and looked down on when they're celebrated for it. The double standard drives me absolutely nuts.

Settling into my seat beside Cari, I take in the arena's atmosphere. There's nothing like being immersed in the furor and frenzy of a hockey game.

"You mind if we take a photo together?" she asks, lifting her phone.

Shaking my head, I pose and smile, and she snaps the picture. I watch as she tags me in the photo before posting it online. My phone buzzes in my pocket.

"So, what's the deal with you and my brother?" Cari asks. Somehow, I don't think she's talking about Al…

I squeak. "There's no deal."

She hums. "I don't believe you."

"You don't have to believe me," I splutter. "There's nothing going on."

Cari looks me up and down, her face saying enough.

"It's *nothing*," I stress.

"I thought it was weird that Al didn't want to pursue anything, but seeing you with Tony…" She shakes her head. "I don't know. Maybe I'm just hoping. I've always wanted a sister."

"I have two. Do you want them?" I joke.

But from the way her lips form a thin line, I don't think she finds the humor.

"When your brothers are ready to settle down, they'll find partners," I say instead. "There's nothing going on—with either of your brothers."

She gives a little pout. "I know, I know. You've made it clear. I was just hoping."

"Hey." Turning in my seat, I set my hand on her arm and

wait for her to meet my eyes. "You have twenty-five players on our squad who will happily be your sisters. You have teammates now. That bond can't be broken."

Cari gives me a tremulous smile. "Really?"

"We won't always get along, we'll get on each other's nerves, but with teams like ours, we'll be there for you through thick and thin." I grin at her. "Being in this league, it's different from when you played in college. It's not just for fun anymore, it's not a hobby. It's work. What we do matters. We have a good time, yeah, but we're there because we want to be, because we want to grow the sport. We support one another."

"I see that," she says quietly. "I'm really seeing that."

Squeezing her arm, I give her a smile. "I'm glad you're on our team."

"Me too," she says, her eyes wet.

She clears her throat a few times as we focus our attention back on the game in front of us. The score is tied, 2-2, and Montreal is giving Boston a run for their money.

"So, where is Tony tonight?" I ask casually. "I thought he'd be here with you."

Cari raises her eyebrows. "Really? Why?"

"No reason," I hurry to add.

"He's at work."

"At the animal shelter?"

"No, the restaurant. He's a waiter at this high-end place in the North End," she says. "He only works at the shelter part-time."

"Plus training."

"Yeah. He's on the men's national gymnastics team," she says proudly. "He's in the running to go to the World Championships in Rotterdam in a few weeks."

"Really?" My voice goes up. "That's super cool."

"He went to the Olympics three years ago, brought home a bronze medal."

Like I didn't Google him the second I found out his name. Well, *after* my panic attack.

Beside me down the row, I see Sadie and Rachel listening to us, amused. Vanessa and Hailey, on the other end, are obliviously paying attention to the hockey game.

"I'm kind of surprised you didn't meet there," Cari continues. "You were there, right?"

"There were a lot of people on Team USA," I deflect.

She hums as two hockey players collide against the boards in front of us. I like that she doesn't otherwise react to the giant crash. She's used to this, same as I am. It's par for the course when your sibling grows up in hockey. They crash into *everything*.

"It's kind of cool that you're meeting now. Maybe you can be friends," she says with the endless optimism of someone who has never had an awkward encounter with their ex.

Not that Tony is my ex. It was just one time. That's all it was.

That's all it will ever be

"Yeah, maybe," I echo quietly.

Sadie reaches over, handing me a bucket of popcorn. "We're going to a bar after the game," she announces. "You coming with?"

"The rest of the team will be there?" I ask.

She nods. "You know, the usual place."

Smart of her not to say the bar's name when we're mixed in with everyone. Even though we get into the VIP section, we don't need the rest of the arena trying to come party with us. Personal safety is a major concern.

"Yeah, I'm in," I decide. "Cari, you coming?"

She nods. "Al already told me we'll ride home together."

"Great," Sadie echoes. "Jared has an early morning meeting, so we won't be staying out too late."

The Grizzlies manage to pull off a win with a sneaky goal late in the third period, and as we wait for the crowd to filter out, I open my phone and pull up the photo Cari tagged me in. There are several thousand likes and a few hundred comments.

A text scrolls across my screen. It's from Alycia.

Let's talk, she's texted, along with a screenshot of the photo.

My stomach drops. Oh no. What did I do?

thirteen

. . .

Viv

THE BAR IS LOUD, packed with people. I feel vaguely claustrophobic. Cari's hand in mine, Rachel's in the other, don't help matters.

Vanessa leads us into the VIP section at the back of the bar. A cocktail waitress comes over to take drink orders and I order a Coke when all my friends order mixed drinks.

I don't care if they drink alcohol. I can be around it just fine. I just don't want to drink it myself.

Hailey went to meet her brother; she didn't come to the bar with us. Now that I think about it, I don't think she's ever come to the bar after a game, and I can't recall ever seeing MacGregor here, either. She's twenty-five and he's twenty-eight, so it's not a matter of not being allowed in. I think it's something else.

Cari leans over to me, her arm around my back as she puts her mouth by my ear. "I like your friends," she says.

Laughing, I grin back at her. "Good. I'm glad."

Although her initial perkiness rubbed me the wrong way, now that I've been around her week in and week out, I know that's just the way she is. Bubbly and effervescent, she can't help brightening everything around her. It's the complete antithesis of what I believe in, but hey, it works for her.

A commotion echoes through the bar as the players descend upon us. Sven Larsson, Jake Lewis, and Jared Aviyente reach our table easily, followed by a tall guy with shaggy, dark brown hair and chocolate brown eyes. I recognize him immediately.

Alberto Gonzales.

My palms get sweaty and my heart skips a beat.

Why am I nervous? He's just another dude bro.

Except he's more than that. He's Cari's brother, yes, but he's also *Tony's* brother. It's important that I get this right.

Al reaches us with a relaxed smile. He stops in front of his sister and pulls her into a hug. "You made it," he says, his voice deep and hoarse.

"Wouldn't miss it for the world," Cari says to him. "This is Viv."

I hurry to my feet, offering my hand for a shake.

Al takes it, tugging me into a hug. "It's nice to finally meet you."

"I'm sorry about… you know." My face heats.

"Bailing on our date?" Al grins at me, his eyes bright. "Don't worry about it. Blind dates are tough."

"Can I buy you a drink?" I offer. "To make up for it?"

"I've got it." He glances at his sister. "You need anything?"

She shakes her head, holding up her full glass. "I'm good."

Al laughs. I don't think his smile has dropped since he walked into the bar. He's like Cari, upbeat and happy.

How did Tony turn out to be so grumpy when both of his siblings are so bubbly and positive? And *why* is his perpetual grumpiness so much more attractive?

As a cocktail waitress comes over to take his order, Al slides into the seat across from me.

"Tell me about yourself," he says.

I laugh. "What do you want to know?"

"Still messy?" His eyes crinkle at me.

That was the excuse I gave him. It would be too messy to date him with our shared connection to his sister.

"Still messy," I echo, my smile fading.

With him, it's easy to turn him down. With his brother… my gut churns. *Why* did he show up to my practice today?

Al shakes his head. "Guess we're going to have to be friends, then."

"Yep. Friends."

There's no spark, no sizzle. I don't want to get him naked. I don't want to know more about him. There's just… nothing.

"Tony mentioned he went to your practice this morning," he says, casually sipping his beer.

"Oh?" My heart skips a beat.

"He says you guys are looking good out there."

He was talking about the team—not me specifically. I try to hide my disappointment.

"Cari's been playing amazing," I deflect. "She's fit into the team perfectly."

"Good. I'm glad."

His sister, talking to someone else on her other side, either can't hear him or isn't paying attention.

"How's your brother doing?" Al asks casually.

I lift my eyebrows. "I have three of them."

He laughs. "The hockey player one. We're playing Colorado next month. Any intel you can give me?"

"None that you can't find out from watching his game tape," I laugh.

That reminds me though—I should probably talk to him. Fuck, I should probably talk to all of my siblings. I don't keep in touch nearly as often as I should. Only Frankie and Bradley are still in school, with Chuck, Perry, and Janine all scattered about doing professional athletics in different cities.

Firing off a quick text in the sibling group chat, I close my phone and set it on the sticky tabletop.

A few other hockey players have approached while I was distracted. I smile at Robby Andrews, who grew up playing hockey with Chuck and now works as the Grizzlies' equipment manager. He squeezes my shoulder, dropping a brief kiss to my cheek, as he scoots past our table.

"You and Andrews?" Al asks, nodding toward him.

I shake my head. "Just friends. I've known him forever."

He hums. "So if you're not interested in me or in Andrews, what's your type?"

My face heats. "Pass."

"No pass. Tell me," he says with a laid-back grin, sinking back into his chair. "We'll find you someone."

"I'm not really looking."

Al laughs. "That's when you find 'em."

"What about you? You looking?"

To my surprise, his sigh is heavy. "Yeah. I'm over the whole hookup scene. I'm ready for what they have." He nods toward Jake and Rachel, who are making out, and Sven and Vanessa, who are talking quietly with each other, lost in their own little world.

Reaching out, I squeeze his hand. I'm not sure why I feel the need to comfort him. I barely know him. Still, something calls in me to take care of him. He's too pure for this world.

"Your time will come," I tell him seriously.

He lifts a shoulder. "Someday my princess will come."

It takes me a second to place the reference. "I didn't take you for a Snow White fan," I tease.

"Cari loved all the Disney princesses growing up," he says defensively. "She got first dibs on the TV being the only girl."

But once he meets my eyes and sees I'm laughing *with* him, not *at* him, he relaxes a bit.

I like Al. I still don't have any feelings for him, I definitely don't want to date him, but hanging out? I think I can manage that.

As the night winds down, my friends and his teammates start to leave.

"Do you want a ride?" he asks as he reaches for his coat.

"Nah, I'll catch an Uber."

"You sure?" Cari pipes in, looking over at us. She's been chatting with some of the other players all night. "We have room in the car."

"Yeah. I'm good." I give her a smile that actually feels genuine. "I had a nice time tonight. I'm glad we went out."

"Me too."

To my surprise, she launches herself at me, wrapping me in a hug. It takes me a second to catch my breath and wrap my arms around her.

"We're friends. Right?" She looks at me hopefully with big doe eyes.

"Yeah. Of course."

She's my teammate. That automatically makes her my friend. Isn't that how it works?

"I'm so glad," Cari says happily. "This is going to be great."

fourteen

. . .

Tony

MY STOMACH SINKS as I stare at the photo. Al and Cari, with Vivienne sandwiched between them. His smile is genuine. Hers too. I can tell because she's never once looked at me that way.

Flicking to the next photo, my heart stops. Because it's a group of couples. Al and Cari are there with Vivienne again, of course, with her friends and their boyfriends. I recognize Sven Larsson and Jake Lewis, along with two of her friends from the bar. There's another couple—the woman with the nose ring, so her boyfriend must be the team's reporter.

My stomach churns.

This is why she should have gone out with Al. They're much more suited. They have more in common.

"You moping again?" Susan's voice cuts through my thoughts.

"I'm fine," I tell her, shoving my phone back into my pocket.

"C'mon. Tell me what's going on with you," she says, tugging me by my hoodie into the office.

Collapsing onto the threadbare armchair opposite her

desk, I sigh and run my hand through my hair. It's starting to grow out again; it's almost time for a cut.

"Is it work? Or training?" Susan asks.

"Neither. Both?" Slumping lower in the chair, I glare at her. "All I do is work and train. I don't have time for anything else."

She knows about my other job and my gymnastics; she has to, because she helps me schedule around my other commitments.

"Do you need some time off?"

I shake my head. "I'm already taking time off for Worlds." If I make the team, that is.

"You can take some more time," she says hesitantly.

We both know the shelter runs on bare-bones staffing. It's not fair to the other staff and volunteers if I take any more time off when I'm perfectly capable of working. I'd rather save the special favors for when I truly need them.

"I'm worried about you," Susan says. "You're going to burn out."

"I just—I need *something*," I tell her honestly. "I've been trying for some brand partnerships. Nobody wants me to endorse their products. I don't know what to post on social media. Both Al and Cari are so much better at it than me."

"Can you ask them for help?" She nudges me. "Maybe your fans want to see who you are."

Choking out a laugh, I shake my head. "Who am I? I don't even know that."

Shadow, hiding in my hoodie pocket, sticks out her little head and gives a soft meow.

Susan laughs. "Has she been there this entire time?"

I nod. "She doesn't let me put her down for very long."

She's growing fast. I won't be able to carry her around in my hoodie for much longer.

"You're going to spoil that damn kitten," she says with a

smile. "What are you going to do with her while you're at Worlds?"

With a sigh, I gently stroke the top of the kitten's head. "I don't know."

"You know as well as I do that separation anxiety like hers gets worse, not better. You're prolonging the inevitable."

"I just don't want to disappoint her," I admit.

Susan pins me with her stare. "She's a cat. She'll get over it."

With a soft grunt, I don't disagree. Doesn't mean it's not on my mind.

As I do a new adoption intake and help a dog find their new forever home, I can't help but wish I had that too. I love living with my siblings in our childhood house, but I don't feel at home there. It's just a place to live. Too much of my life is in flux—the upcoming end of my gymnastics career, not knowing if I'll apply to vet school this year.

The bell above the door chimes, and I force myself to leave the back room and head into the lobby. We don't get a lot of adoption inquiries this late in the day, mainly people whose pets have gone missing, and there haven't been any new arrivals in the last forty-eight hours.

But when I see the person in our lobby, my mouth goes dry.

Vivienne is hovering awkwardly at the end of the reception desk, her hands tucked into her jacket pockets. Her hair is tied up in a ponytail, light makeup on her face. She's wearing dark jeans, a soft cotton T-shirt, and a lightweight puffer jacket with knee-length black boots. Effortlessly casual but put together at the same time.

She looks absolutely fucking gorgeous.

"What are you doing here?" The words come out before I can pull them back.

An awkward smile tilts her lips. "Isn't that my line?"

My stomach flips at the lack of vitriol in her voice. I choke out a laugh. "Yeah. I think so."

She swallows, apprehension on her face. "I was wondering…"

Impatiently, I wait for her to finish her sentence. "Yeah?"

She looks at something over my shoulder, like she can't quite bring herself to meet my eyes.

"Is that offer for coffee still on the table?"

"Yes," I say immediately.

Her eyes dart to mine, then away.

"Yes, coffee," I repeat dumbly. "Um, my shift—"

I still have two and a half hours on the clock.

"Oh. Right." Vivienne shakes her head. "It doesn't have to be now, I guess. It can be… whenever."

"Now's good." Susan's voice behind me makes me jump. "Tony, get out of here. I can handle the rest of the day."

"Are you sure?" My voice cracks.

My boss nods. "I'm good. Go ahead and clock out."

I give Vivienne a small smile. "Give me two minutes?"

She nods, turning to study the wall of photos—successful adoptions. Whenever I'm in a bad mood, I look at that wall of pictures.

Following Susan into the backroom, I glare at my meddling boss. "What's that about?"

"You need this," she says, squeezing my shoulder. "Leave Shadow here. You go out with that pretty little thing and take a load off."

My eyebrows go up. "Excuse me?"

"You're going to burn out," she says, same as she did a few hours ago. "You need a break. Seems like she'll be good for you."

"It's just coffee," I mutter as I swipe my employee badge at the scanner to clock out.

Oh shit. I pull up short.

Coffee.

With Vivienne.

While I'm wearing sweaty, animal hair-covered clothes.

Ducking into the employee bathroom, I quickly wash my hands and face. My hoodie smells a bit ripe and is covered in cat hair, so I swap it for a mostly clean zip-up with the shelter logo from my locker. It's not like I keep an entire wardrobe here.

I stare at myself in the mirror. Exacerbated by the shitty lighting, I can see the exhaustion on my face. I only have a few hours before I have to head to the steakhouse for another grueling night of serving overpriced food to the privileged elite.

My phone is burning a hole in my pocket, and I pull it out to stare at the photo again. She may have gone out with Al last night, but today, she's reaching out to me. I have to see this through.

Vivienne is waiting in the lobby, and as I approach, shrugging on my leather jacket, she looks me up and down. Something bright shines in her eyes. Is it appreciation? I certainly hope so.

"There's a coffee shop down the block," I say casually. "Does that work?"

She nods. "Lead the way."

I set a light hand on her lower back on reflex as I escort her outside. She doesn't flinch away, so I take it as a sign that maybe she doesn't hate me quite so much as she used to. I don't know what I did to change that, but I'll take it.

I'll take anything she gives me.

Inside the coffee shop, we wait silently in line, but the silence isn't oppressive. She orders a black coffee and pays before I can get to the card reader, then waits at the end of the bar as I order myself a green tea. We receive our drinks and make our way to a small table in the corner.

"So…" I stare at her from across the table. "You wanted to talk?"

Vivienne scowls, but it's missing her usual heat. "You invited me for coffee."

"Yeah. And you turned me down." I try hard to keep the bitterness out of my voice, but I don't think I'm successful.

She looks away.

"Did… something change?"

She takes a deep breath. "So it turns out you *aren't* a total scumbag."

My stomach drops with disappointment. Though I try to keep my expression neutral, I don't think I'm successful. "Is that what you thought of me?"

"I used to," she says steadily.

When I don't react, she sighs.

"Not really," she admits. "I was hurt and angry. I was taking it out on you, and you didn't do anything to deserve it."

I swallow. "Why were you hurt?"

Her eyes flash, and my stomach tenses in anticipation.

fifteen

. . .

Viv

THIS IS HARD TO SAY.

"You left," I say quietly. "The morning after…"

He pauses. "I messaged you."

My eyebrows go up. "No, you didn't."

"Yeah. I had to leave—I had to get to practice—but I sent you a DM on Instagram. I knew it was a long shot," he adds. "But I was hoping you'd see it."

"My socials are all locked down, especially that summer." Anticipation flutters in my stomach. "You messaged me?"

"Yeah. I tried to find you at the Closing Ceremony, but there were too many people. And then we came back home and you were on the talk show circuit, and I had the tour, and…" He trails off. "I had fun. I wanted to do it again."

I shake my head to clear my thoughts. "Have you lived in Boston all this time?" This is my fifth season with the Revolution; I've been here ever since.

He nods.

"Why haven't you reached out again?"

Tony laughs. "Hello, stalker, much? It was a one-night stand three years ago. I didn't want you to think I was some creep. You didn't answer, I left it at that. I figured you weren't interested."

Disappointment flows through me. "I wish I'd known who you were."

He blinks. "You didn't remember me?"

Is that judgment in his voice?

"Not by name," I admit. "I…"

His foot nudges mine under the table. He presses his shoe against mine.

"I woke up that morning, used and hungover, and decided to make some changes in my life. I haven't had a drink since." My eyes are on my coffee cup. I can't bring myself to look at him, see the pity or derision on his face. I don't think I'd be able to survive it if he looked at me with disgust.

Tony reaches across the table and tips my chin up.

"That's something to be proud of," he says quietly.

"Really?" My voice comes out in a croak.

"I'm proud of you," he says seriously.

My heart skips a beat.

"Too many people have a problem and don't let themselves address it. You did. You decided enough was enough and tackled it head on. That's admirable." His eyes hold mine. "I'm proud of you."

I didn't know how much I needed to hear that. Not necessarily from *him*, but in general. I don't talk about the *why* I stopped drinking with most people. It's personal, intertwined with our history. I don't particularly enjoy being flayed alive with all my nerve endings exposed.

But with him… being vulnerable doesn't feel like the worst thing in the world.

"I've tried to go to meetings, but they don't—I don't fit in there," I admit. "They all talk about a higher power and for me… it didn't click."

"So you've just been white-knuckling it ever since?" His mouth turns up in a half-smile.

"Something like that." I don't consider myself an addict or an alcoholic. I was perfectly capable of stopping. "I didn't like the person I became when I drank."

Tony reaches out and knocks his cup of tea against my coffee cup. "I like the person you are now."

All the air whooshes out of me. "You do?"

He nods, and though his smile is casual, there's a tension in his shoulders that makes me curious as to its cause.

"I didn't like that you hated me. When Cari joined the Revolution, I hoped our paths would cross again."

My face falls at the mention of his sister. "They did."

He swallows, his Adam's apple bobbing in the thick column of his throat. "Do you still hate me?"

Not as much as I hate myself.

"The animosity has decreased lately." I offer him an over-the-top cheesy smile.

Tony barks out a laugh. "Good. I'm glad."

"I went out with Al last night." I say the words in a rush. "Well, not *out*, out, we were at the same place at the same time and we hung out."

His eyebrows go up. "I know."

"He told you?" My stomach sinks. Here I was hoping to navigate this sibling thing easily…

"I saw the photos Cari posted online," he says, glancing away.

"Oh."

"Do you… are you and him…" He trails off. "If you wanted to date him, I'd understand. He's a catch."

Shaking my head, I wait for him to meet my eyes. "There's nothing there."

"Because you were supposed to go out with him," Tony adds quickly. "So I'd get it if—"

"There's only one Gonzales sibling that interests me," I tell him. My heart pounds rapid-fire.

His eyes dart to mine, then away again. "Cari, then?"

"Not your sister."

This time, when his rich brown eyes meet mine, there's a quiet vulnerability shining in their depths.

"I'm sorry for being a dick to you when we first met," I say quietly. "I was hurt. Seeing you again... it brought up a lot of bad memories, things I hadn't properly dealt with."

"And have you?" he asks. "Dealt with them?"

"I'm working on it," I admit. "I'd like a do-over."

Slowly, a brilliant smile spreads across his face. "Hey. I'm Tony. It's nice to see you again." He holds his hand out for a shake.

"I'm Viv." Sliding my hand into his feels like coming home.

Tony flips my hand over, tracing his thumb over my palm. "Vivienne."

I shake my head. "No. Call me Viv."

To my surprise, he presses a kiss to my palm. "You've always been Vivienne to me."

My breath catches.

Then Tony grimaces. "I don't have a lot of free time, but I'd like to take you out. Properly, this time."

"I can make that happen. Cari said you work in the North End?"

He nods. "Yeah. Between there, the shelter, and training, I don't have a lot of time for myself, much less for another person."

"How did you get started at the shelter?" When he pauses, I add in quickly: "You don't have to tell me."

"I've been volunteering there since high school," Tony finally says. "I want to go to vet school."

"That's awesome!"

His small smile is pained. "Yeah, well, in order to do that, I need to retire."

Oh.

"There's no way to do gymnastics while you're in school?"

He shakes his head. "It takes up too much time. And my body's giving up on me." His lips quirk into a half-smile. "I've already decided to retire after I turn thirty."

"Oh? When's that?"

"March. They'll name next summer's Olympic team at the national championships in June, but I don't know if I'm going to push for that," Tony admits quietly. "I just…"

I glance around the coffee shop, but nobody is paying attention to us. "After the Olympics next summer, I'm done," I tell him, just as quietly.

As long as I stay healthy and keep to my regular standard of play, I'm a shoo-in for the team, or so Alycia says. I'm certainly not ready to be *done* entirely. I want one more chance to prove my worth and bring that gold medal home. If I fail, I fail, but I'll have done it knowing I've given the sport my all.

His eyes snap to mine.

"My contract with the Revolution expires at the end of the season and I'm not going to renew it. I've already decided I want to move on to something new." I laugh awkwardly. "I don't know what it'll be yet, just that it'll be something different."

Tony gulps loudly. "I'm guessing this isn't public knowledge."

I shake my head. "Only my agent knows. I haven't told the team or my friends. I haven't even told my family."

His mouth moves wordlessly for a few moments. "Thank you for your trust in me. I won't share this with anyone."

"I know you won't." I'm not sure how I know, just that I do.

Me and him, we're two sides of the same coin. On the

precipice of change, the world is open to us, and it feels so fucking daunting to know I can do anything I want to. Maybe I'll travel the world, maybe I'll stay put, maybe I'll move across the country. There's no limit to what I can do.

Tony's phone buzzes with an alarm, and he grimaces as he goes to silence it.

"I have to get to work," he says, disappointment in his voice.

I glance at my watch, surprised how three hours have flown by. It feels like we just sat down, but we've been talking forever. It's surprisingly easy to talk to him. He's not the asshole I thought he was. Maybe I was too quick to judge.

"Thanks for meeting with me."

He gives me a crooked smile. "Maybe we could do this again?"

My stomach flutters. "I'd like that."

"I'll call you," he says. He unlocks his phone and hands it to me to punch in my number. I call myself so I have his number too. "How does Monday night work?"

"Wow. You really mean it." Even though I knew he was interested, I didn't think he'd actually go so far as to make plans right away. I thought I'd have to work for it a little more.

His dark eyes are bright when he grins at me, softening his features. "I don't want you to change your mind."

"I won't," I promise. "Monday night is great."

Tony leans into my personal space and I get a whiff of his spicy sandalwood scent. He presses a soft kiss on my cheek.

"I can't wait."

sixteen

. . .

Tony

"FOR FUCK'S SAKE, shut up already," Al snaps at me from across the kitchen table.

It's a rare occasion when my brother and I are home at the same time. Even more rare that we actually spend time together.

I've been whistling for the last three days, ever since Vivienne agreed to go out with me. Tonight's the night. I have it all planned out.

"What are you so happy about, anyway?" Al demands.

"Got a date tonight." I grin as I scramble half a dozen eggs for the both of us.

"Good for you. Now shut up."

Laughing, I lean against the counter and wait for the eggs to cook.

"It's been a while, hasn't it?" Al asks.

"She was worth waiting for."

"Do I know her?"

My heart stops for a second. Vivienne and I didn't discuss if we were letting people know. We're too connected. What if it doesn't work out? What if she decides I'm too much of a grumpy asshole for her after all? I don't think I'd be able to handle all of our friends and my family asking what went wrong.

"Nah, you don't know her," I lie, stirring the eggs.

"Well, I'm leaving for a road trip, so you just have to deal with Cari tonight," Al says. "You might want to warn her to clear out and give you some space."

"I'm not going to bring her back here."

My brother raises his eyebrows. "You're not?"

"Not for a first date, at least," I amend. "We'll see how it goes."

Also, I'm fairly sure Vivienne lives alone. Best case scenario, we can go to her place... but I'm not banking on anything happening. I like her too much to jeopardize what we could have. I'm interested in more than sex with her. That means not rushing into things.

Al shrugs and rolls his eyes, putting his attention back to his phone.

"What about you?" I force myself to ask. "Seeing anyone?"

My brother's eyes widen. "Since when do you care?"

"I don't. I'm making conversation." My chin lifts. "Forget it."

To my surprise, he grins. "I'm not seeing anyone. All of my teammates are settling down and I... I want what they have, you know? I want my forever person."

"You're still young. You have time."

Al shrugs. "I don't think age factors into it. I'm ready for something serious." He pauses. "It turns out when you go into it with the intention of serious, it kind of scares women off. Like I'm putting them on a penalty kill when we're down by two in the last five minutes of the third."

"Pressure cooker." I nod, turning off the burner and scooping eggs onto two plates already loaded with black beans, sliced avocado, and tortillas. The pico de gallo I made earlier is already on the table. "I can see how that might be too intense for a first date."

He nods. "I don't want to fuck around anymore. I want a relationship that actually means something."

"I get that."

"You do?" He laughs. "Mr. Grumpy McGrumperson wants an actual relationship?"

Shrugging, I let myself admit the truth. "With her, I think I do."

Al whistles. "Shit. You like her."

"I really do."

He claps me on the shoulder. "When do we get to meet her?"

I ignore the fact that he's already met her. "How about after we have our first few dates?"

"Yeah, it might be too soon." Al laughs. "I'm happy for you, Tone. Really."

Buoyant, I carry that with me all day at training and throughout my shift at the shelter. Brody is amused, Coach less so, but when I stick my vault again and again and again, he certainly can't complain. Well, not any more than usual. Coach wouldn't be Coach if he didn't complain.

———

Vivienne lives in a squat, three-story brownstone in Weymouth, not far from where the Revolution play in Quincy. She's waiting on the sidewalk when I pull up on my motorcycle. A smile stretches from ear to ear.

"Hey." I greet her with a smile of my own. Swinging my leg over the side of the bike, I approach her and give her a soft kiss on the cheek. "You look great."

She's wearing tight, dark jeans, a blood-red sweater, and a black bomber jacket. Her dark brown hair is loose around her shoulders with a subtle wave that I'm sure probably took forever to achieve. Although her makeup is light and natural, her dark red lipstick does dangerous things to my heart rate.

Then again, being around her in general makes my heart pound like crazy.

"Thanks. You clean up pretty good yourself."

I can't deny her words make me feel good. I've shaved and taken care styling my hair, although it probably got messed up by my helmet, and I was deliberate picking out my clothes. Cari says women go wild for a guy in a Henley. I want to look good for her. I want her to be confident to show up on my arm.

Grabbing the spare helmet from the storage compartment on my bike, I hand it over, and as she tugs it over her head, my cock twitches at the sight of her in my gear.

As I step closer to her, I catch a whiff of her sweet strawberry perfume. I quickly check the fit on her helmet, making sure she's secured.

"Have you ridden a motorcycle before?" I ask, swinging my leg over.

Vivienne shakes her head. "First time for everything."

I like that we can have some firsts together. Helps make up for our negative first time.

"Climb on behind me and wrap your arms around my waist."

Her eyes brighten teasingly as she does so, and a shiver goes through me at the innocent contact. "Like this?"

Her hands settle innocently on my obliques. I can feel the heat of her through my shirt and jacket.

My mouth goes dry. "Yeah. That's… that's good."

It takes me a few moments to regroup before I turn the bike back on and pull out into traffic.

Navigating the streets of Boston is second nature for me. I grew up here, and aside from my four years at Berkeley, I've spent my entire adult life here. Driving through the city with a gorgeous woman on my bike? I've never experienced anything like this.

Dinner and drinks are the cliché first date, so that's exactly what I didn't want. It's a little chilly for a picnic. A museum feels stuffy. There are so many historical places in the city to sight-see, but that didn't feel right, either. Any sort of physical activity like ice skating is definitely not allowed, not when I'm this close to Worlds selection, and she's in training.

So when we pull up to the Boston Garden, I can see her confusion and disappointment when she takes off her helmet.

"You brought me to a hockey game?"

"Basketball." I hold my breath. "It's something neither of us have any ties to, I don't know anyone on the team, and it's better than staring awkwardly at each other from across a table."

To my surprise, she cracks a grin. "I dig it."

She hands me the helmet to stow it away, and then before I know what's happened, she's grabbing my hand and lacing our fingers together.

"If you brought me to see your brother play, I'd have been disappointed," she admits. "We can do that anytime."

"Your friends are connected to the team. It wouldn't be special. I wanted something for us, but still casual."

Her eyebrows arch up. "Is that what you're looking for? Casual?"

"I didn't want to take you to a fancy restaurant that reminds me of my job," I tell her honestly. "I can bring you Michelin-starred food any night you want. Eating that way is not part of my diet plan, at least right now."

"Because you're gearing up for a competition."

"World championships." I nod. As we approach the check stand, I scan our tickets to gain entry, then take her hand again. "I have a pretty good shot of making the team. There are five spots, plus two alternates. The team needs my vault score to make the finals."

"I don't know much about gymnastics," Vivienne says. "The basics, yeah. Simone Biles is the greatest of all the time. Maybe it makes me a bad athlete."

"Not at all. I didn't know anything about rugby before the last Olympics."

She smiles, but it doesn't reach her eyes. "Yeah? Did us bringing home the silver medal change that?"

"Nope." I tug on her hand until she turns to face me. "You did."

seventeen

. . .

Viv

OUR SEATS ARE in the upper level in the middle of a row. I like that Tony didn't try to use his brother's connections to get prime seats or spots in a suite. I've got connections of my own. Asking for favors doesn't impress me. People have used me enough; I won't stand for anyone else to be used, either. Maybe some people would want to be treated that way, but I'm more interested in getting to know *him*, not what he can do for me.

The protein options at the arena are rather lacking, so we both settle for chicken sandwiches and agree to split a soft pretzel as our cheat treat. He waves off my offer to pay, settling his hand on my lower back as we walk back to our seats.

"Are you a big basketball fan?" I ask as we get comfortable.

Tony laughs. "Not really. I watch a few games here and there."

"And yet you brought me here?"

He grins. "I mean, I like it. The guys and I will shoot hoops after training. It's more I think other sports are more fun to watch."

"I haven't been to a game in forever. Not since… maybe three years ago?" I try to recall. "Perry was still here, he dragged me."

"Who's Perry?" There's a little furrow above his brow that I want to smooth away with my thumb. Somehow, I resist. Touching people without their consent is bad.

"My brother. One of them," I explain. "He was signed with New England for a few years when I first moved here, then he got traded to Raleigh."

"This is the football player?"

My eyes narrow, but I can't keep my smile off my face. "Did you Google me?"

Like he's playing at nonchalant, he shrugs, but he can't hide the smile on his lips. "Maybe."

A warm shiver of happiness runs through me. He cared enough to look me up. He wanted to know more about me.

"Yeah. Perry's the football player. Chuck does hockey."

"For Denver," he says slowly, like he's trying to remember.

I nod.

"And the rest?"

"Janine is a swimmer at the national training facility out in Colorado, Frankie is a volleyball player at Clemson, and Bradley… he doesn't do sports." I take a bite of the pretzel. It's soft and doughy and *so* not on my diet plan. I take a second bite. "My mom coaches the Clemson volleyball team and my dad works for USA Tennis. That's it. That's my family."

Tony laughs. "It sounds like a lot to keep track of."

"It can be," I allow. "They're overwhelmingly supportive. Sometimes too much."

"My parents are the same way."

"Do they live here? You live with your siblings, right?"

He nods. "They're in Florida, taking care of my *abuela*. The winters here are too harsh for her. After I graduated from college, I came back here. Cari moved in after she graduated last spring, and I keep expecting Al to find his own place, he can afford it, but he seems to like staying with us."

"My brother lived with me when he was here. Well, I lived with him. When he got traded, I found a new place." I shrug. "We're never going to have all six of us under one roof again. Even for things like Thanksgiving and the holidays, we stay in hotels. My parents' three bedroom house can't handle all of us, but outside of one or two weeks a year, they don't need to keep the space. Only the youngest two are still in school. The rest of us are all self-supporting."

Thank goodness for social media endorsements. I earn a comfortable salary from the Revolution, but the majority of my income comes from paid promotion. I don't know what I'll do once I retire next summer, but the pay probably won't be anywhere near enough on its own. And the farther I get from my rugby career, the less draw I'll have for potential advertisers. I'll have to find something else to bring the money in.

"Do you have plans for after retirement?" Tony asks.

I shrug. "Not so much. I still have this upcoming season and next year's Olympics to figure it out."

If we place well at the Games, I can try to go back on the talk show circuit, maybe get on a reality TV show… but it all feels so exhausting. I'm not ready to think about it yet. That's Alycia's job.

"I'm sure you'll have tons of offers."

"Here's hoping." I manage a smile, but it feels forced. "What vet schools are you applying to?"

His face flushes. "I, um, haven't decided yet."

"Are you going to try to stay local?"

Is this thing between us dead on arrival? If he's moving, do I even put in the effort?

"I want to, yeah," Tony says quietly. "My siblings are here. And yeah, I know they can be traded at any time, but it's home." He sighs. "There's only one good vet school in the city, and if I don't get in, I don't think I'd have the stomach to apply again. There are other schools in New England, but it would mean moving out again, and I just…"

"It's a lot."

"Yeah." He looks at me out of the corner of his eye. "This isn't exactly fun date conversation, is it?"

"I'm digging it." Relaxing a bit, I give him a smirk. "I'd much rather you be real with me than pretend to be someone else."

To my surprise, he swallows and nods seriously. His fingertips skim over my cheek. "I'll only ever be real with you."

My heart skips a beat and my mouth goes dry.

"I don't play games," Tony says. "What this is, what we could have… It's important to me. It's *real*."

Before I know what I'm doing, I'm yanking him by his shirt collar and crashing my mouth to his. His body is tense, but his lips are soft and yielding beneath mine.

It takes all of a second for him to react. And then his fingers slide into my hair, cupping the back of my skull in his massive palm, as he kisses me senseless. His tongue slips into my mouth, stroking mine. My entire body turns into goo. I melt against him, or as much as I can in the uncomfortable stadium seat.

There's a shout and then a whistle chirps, and we break apart. I almost forgot about the basketball game going on below us.

Tony doesn't go far. He rests his forehead against mine, breathing hard. His eyes are closed. How have I never noticed how long and thick his eyelashes are? His eyelashes are the goals of every mascara company everywhere.

When I realize I'm still clutching his shirt collar, I release him, smoothing the fabric back into place. He lets out a soft chuckle, plucking my hand away and pressing a soft kiss to my palm.

Easing back into my own personal space bubble, I clear my throat. "Sorry for, um, mauling you."

Tony blinks his eyes open, a hazy smile on his face. "You can maul me anytime."

"You'd probably like that, wouldn't you?" I tease, nudging him with my elbow.

"Yeah," he says, his eyes bright. "I would."

My stomach swoops and drops like I'm on a rollercoaster.

He hasn't made it a secret that he's into me. Now that I've come around… I don't want to hide it, either. I'm too old to play games.

As much as I want to ignore the game and take him back to my place, I know there's no need to rush. He's not going anywhere.

Settling back into my seat, I draw his arm around my shoulders. Tony tightens his arm around me and presses his lips to my hair.

"I like this," he murmurs.

"I like you," I whisper, my eyes trained on the court below. If I turn to look at him and he doesn't feel the same way, I think I might die. If he thinks I'm joking or teasing, I might yeet myself out of this stratosphere.

But Tony just squeezes my arm, his grip reassuring and calm.

"I like you too."

A smile stretches my face from ear to ear, and I have to resist the urge to look at him. From the corner of my eye, I think he's smiling. Good. He's adorable when he's all scowls and frustration, but I like when he smiles. I'm going to do everything in my power to make sure he keeps smiling.

eighteen

· · ·

Tony

I WAKE up to three thousand notifications on my Instagram. My good mood evaporates, just like that.

My first date with Vivienne went great. After her quiet confession in the stands, we watched the rest of the game, trading innocent touches and little kisses. When I drove her home, we parked my bike in front of her building and made out for what felt like forever.

She didn't invite me in and I didn't ask.

And now…

Opening Instagram, I see I've been tagged in a dozen different photos. Most of them are from last night, the two of us at the basketball game, a few shots of us kissing. There's even a photo from when we went to have coffee the other day.

I knew Vivienne was a public figure, but I didn't think she was so well known that people would be essentially stalking her. I really didn't think they'd be able to figure out who *I* *was*, especially not this quickly.

My phone lights up with a call from her, and I answer immediately.

"Good morning." My voice comes out husky and sleep-hoarse.

"I'm so sorry," she blurts.

"Sorry about what?"

"You should check social media," she says. "They're… well, it's everywhere. Our date."

"I saw it. It's fine."

It's *not* fine. I don't enjoy having my privacy violated. But they don't care about me, they're interested in her. As soon as she breaks this off, I'm sure they'll lose interest in me.

Vivienne is quiet. I can hear noise on the other end of the call—it hasn't dropped—but she doesn't say anything.

"Maybe we should cool off for a little while," she finally says.

My stomach drops. Last night, I thought she was interested in seeing where this could go.

"Is that what you want?"

She lets out a noise of frustration. "No. But I don't want you dragged into anything that makes you uncomfortable. Especially when you have Worlds on the line."

"I'm fine, it's fine."

She laughs. "Yeah, you're super convincing."

"I just want to get to know you better," I tell her. "Do I like that people were taking photos of us without our consent? No. Does that make me want to stop dating you? No. I like *you*. I can deal with them as long as it means more time with you."

"Fuck," she whispers.

"What's wrong?"

She sighs. "You're saying everything right. I just…"

"Does this make you change your mind?"

"No. I'm used to this. My agent might care though."

Oh. I hadn't thought about that.

"Would they have an issue with it?" Holding my breath, I run my hand through my hair as I wait.

"I don't know," Vivienne finally says. "My sponsors might."

"Your sponsors might care that you have a boyfriend?"

"Is that what we are?" Her voice is quiet.

"It's where I'd like us to go," I tell her honestly. "I want to date you. I want to be with you."

It's uncomfortable putting myself on the line like this. At the same time, I don't think I could hide anything from her. Open, honest communication is the only way we'll have a chance at doing this.

"I'll have to think about this," she says.

"Take your time. I'm not going anywhere."

We hang up and I go about my morning routine, getting ready for a full day of training before a shift at the steakhouse. I only have a two-hour break in between.

When I get to the kitchen, Cari is at the table, drinking a protein shake and eating a banana. I make a face. I absolutely hate bananas. The smell, the taste… everything about them makes me gag.

"Good morning to you too," my sister says when she sees my grossed out face. "How was your date?"

"It went well."

"Think you're going to see Viv again?"

I stop in my tracks. I didn't tell her who I was going out with, just that I had a date.

"W-who?"

Cari rolls her eyes. "You know, my team captain. The woman you were sucking face with all night?"

She shows me her phone, where there's another photo of us. This one I haven't seen yet. Her tongue is quite obviously in my mouth.

"I'm guessing she doesn't hate you anymore."

"Nope." It doesn't thrill me anymore, not with her having one foot out the door.

Bustling through the kitchen, I start preparing my own protein shake. No bananas.

"Come on. What's that face for?"

"I can't talk to you about this."

"Why not?" Cari asks. "She's my team captain."

"Exactly. You have to work with her. I don't want to make things awkward."

"You won't."

Turning on the blender, I let it whirr. Cari opens her mouth and I press the button again.

"But—"

I drown out her voice until she finally gets the hint and stops talking.

"Don't be a dick, Tone," she says, crossing her arms over her chest. "I just want you to be happy."

"I just want me to be happy too," I mutter as I pour my shake into a glass.

"And Viv makes you happy?"

A beat pulses between us.

"Tony," Cari says firmly. "Does Viv make you happy?"

Slowly, I raise my eyes to hers. There's no anger, just concern.

"I think she could," I tell her quietly.

"Then go after her. Tell her. Show her."

"It's not that easy. She's worried about her career."

"Good. That means she's still grounded in reality," Cari says. "She's not off in la la land. She's thinking about how to make it work. So show her you're in this. Prove that you're serious about her."

I carry my sister's words with me throughout the day. All through training, it's all I can think about. Even when Coach yells at me to get out of my head, I can't seem to bring myself to focus on the here and now.

"What's with you today?" Brody asks when I fall for the third time in five routines on the high bar.

"Got a lot on my mind." Dusting myself off, I head for the chalk bowl and prepare to start again.

"Well, you need to focus. Compartmentalize all of that shit," he says. "World's will be here in a few weeks. They're watching all of our practices ahead of selection camp next week. You've got to be on your game."

"I know, I know."

Nothing he's saying is news to me. I know how this works. Next week, they'll decide who goes to the Worlds Championships and who will go to the other competitions rounding out the rest of the year. I've gone through this process for years. Usually, I'm better at turning my brain off and focusing on the skills.

Today? All I can think of is Vivienne. What if I lose her before we ever have a chance to begin?

nineteen

. . .

Viv

ALYCIA HAS CALLED me twice before nine o'clock in the morning. This is big, because she lives on the west coast, and it's still six o'clock her time. As much as I don't want to talk to her, I think I have to.

What if she tells me to break off this thing with Tony? What if my sponsors pull my funding? Am I strong enough to push back and stand up for myself?

I'd like to think I am. I'd like to think this fledgling thing Tony and I have is worth sacrificing my career for.

So when Alycia calls for the third time, I answer it before it can ring.

"Tell me about the boyfriend," she says immediately.

"It's new."

I can practically hear her eyes roll. "I'm sure it is. Tell me about him."

"What do you want to know?"

She sighs. "Okay, he's your teammate's brother and he's an athlete. Does he have representation?"

"I'm not sure," I say honestly. I'm not surprised she already knows this. She probably has a dossier on everyone in my life.

"Pump It Up is intrigued," Alycia says after a pause. "They'd be interested in doing a feature."

I freeze. "What?"

Pump It Up Protein Powder is one of my biggest sponsors.

"They'd like to pay you to feature some of their products. It would be a series of posts and videos with both of you featured," she says.

"You've already heard from them?"

My agent laughs. "Please. I put out feelers last week, after the photos of you two looking cozy at the coffee shop."

My stomach swoops. "You saw those?"

"I have Google Alerts on all my people," she says dismissively. "I didn't know his name, but when his sister posted a photo of them together and I saw the photos from your animal shelter visit, I put the pieces together. He's cute."

"You still follow my teammates?" I'm hung up on that.

"You know me, I'm thorough."

She is. I cause her infinitely fewer problems now that I've stopped drinking, but they haven't stopped altogether. She's always kept tabs on me through the posts my friends make. Even if they don't tag me, I might still be in the background of what they have going on.

She's far less of a stalker than it sounds. She means well. She's just… overbearing. Prepared for all eventualities.

"So tell me about him," Alycia says.

"Last night was our first date. What do you want to know?"

"You're going to keep seeing him." It's not a question.

"Yeah. I'd like to." I play with a loose thread on my shirt. "I like him."

"Good. Then we'll set up some more photo ops," she decides.

"I don't know if he'd be interested in that."

She makes a noise of frustration. "He's a competitive athlete and a semi-public figure. It's part of the job."

"I get the idea he keeps things pretty close to his chest. Besides, he's preparing for a big competition right now."

"So he probably would like a few thousand dollars from sponsors," she concludes, like it's a done deal. "Let me know if he has a rep I need to coordinate with. Otherwise, I'll send over a contract and he can work with me directly."

"You'd do that?"

"Viv, your social rankings are through the roof." Alycia laughs. "If one date with the guy can get you this many interactions, I can't wait to see what happens after you collab together. This might be the magic key we've been looking for to take your partnerships to the next level. You better hope you don't break up."

My palms start to sweat. "We've been on *one* date."

"I saw the photos. You haven't looked that happy in… months. Maybe years."

"I thought you'd tell me to end it," I admit. "Sponsors don't like women in relationships."

"Oh, Viv." She sighs. "Sponsors don't like women, period. Whether you're single or in a committed partnership, nothing you do will ever make them happy. All you can do is live your life. We'll cherry pick which companies we work with to maximize your earnings potential."

She pauses.

"And P.S., happy women sell better."

With that, she hangs up.

My phone buzzes with a message from Kiana. *Where are you?*

With a sigh, I pull on my hoodie and leave my apartment, jogging to the park where we're meeting for a run. She's waiting by the fountain, stretching with Andi and Grace. To my surprise, Cari is with them.

"Good morning," she chirps. I freeze, and my teammates burst into laughter at the stricken look on my face.

"Morning." I glare at them.

"So when's the wedding?" Andi teases.

"Fuck off," I mutter, pulling out my ponytail and retying it. "Are we here to do this or what?"

Technically, it's our day off from training. We could just go out to brunch and call it a day.

"Or what," Kiana echoes. "I'd much rather get all the gossip."

"There is no gossip." I side-eye Cari. "Nothing to tell."

"She's in love with my brother," she says brightly.

I bluster. "It's—we've—we're—"

"I know, it was your first date." She pats me on the arm. "That's what he said too."

"This is too weird." I scrub my hands over my face. "I didn't think this through."

"Are you going to back out?" Grace asks.

"No." I don't have to look at Cari to know she's smiling at my emphatic denial. "I like him. I just have to hope he'll put up with my bullshit."

"He will," Cari says confidently.

"You don't know that."

"He will," she repeats. "He likes you too. You should have seen him all last week. He was disgustingly cheerful."

"Really?" That makes me inordinately happy.

"Oh, yeah. He's smitten." She shakes her head. "I should have known something was up when he came to practice last week. He would never have come to visit me on his own."

I open my mouth.

"Oh, no, I'm not complaining. He's just transparent," Cari laughs. "I deal with him enough at home. He doesn't need to be dropping by our training facility to see me."

My face heats.

"Come on, let's get our workout on," Kiana says. "Then we can mock Viv some more after."

I flip her off and she laughs, setting her headphones over

her ears. Everyone else prepares and then we set off for our run, twice around the five-mile loop.

Running between Kiana and Cari, I lose myself in the physicality of the exercise. Distance running is not my forte, but it helps us train our endurance for the short, quick bursts of speed we need on the pitch.

We complete our loops without further incident and then cool down with a brisk walk. With my headphones on in a clear don't talk to me message, my teammates leave me alone —for now.

To my surprise, they don't bring up Tony as we debate brunch spots or as we make our way to the restaurant. They're almost silent as we place our orders.

So, of course, as soon as I let my guard down, they pounce.

"How long has this been going on?" Kiana demands. "I thought you weren't interested in him."

"I thought you hated him," Grace tacks on.

Grabbing my water glass, I gulp it down.

"I almost feel bad for setting you up with Al," Cari says. "Is that why you ran out?"

"Wait—she set you up with her brother?" Andi says, looking between us. "You went out with both brothers?"

"I didn't realize they were related," I admit.

Cari frowns. "But—wait—"

"I met Tony at the Olympics three years ago." My face flames. "We went our separate ways and didn't reconnect very well."

Her eyes go wide. "You're his bronze medal."

"What? No."

"He's talked about you for the last three years. I didn't know she was you!"

I bury my face in my hands.

Cari goes on: "They met the night before the team final. He says you're the reason he won the bronze medal."

"He's exaggerating," I deflect.

"My brother… he's not good with people. He's hard for other people to read," she says slowly. "But when he lets you into his world? There's nothing better."

"I like him. I want to see where it goes." That's one thing I'm sure of. "I just don't want to scare him off."

"He doesn't scare easily," Cari says. "Give him some credit. Give him a chance."

"I will."

I just have to hope he'll give me one too.

twenty

. . .

Tony

DESPITE SOME EARLY DISTRACTIONS, once I was able to screw my head on straight, it turned into one of my best trainings of the past few weeks. It couldn't have come at a better time; Ross, the national team coordinator, is at the training facility today.

After a break for lunch, Ross sets us into a mini competition. He wants to see our final routines, not just the bits and pieces we're training. There are sixteen men on the national team plus another eight on the senior developmental team who have the potential to be named in the next year if their scores are up to snuff. Only nine of us train here at the national team's facility; the rest are throughout the country, some are still in college or high school, at the gyms of their choice.

One bonus of training year round at the national team's campus? We get more eyes on us. When Ross wants to see our progress, he can do it in person and not through a shaky video recorded on the coaches' phones. We get extra chances for visibility ahead of formal selection camps, like the one coming up next week. Even though it technically will all come down to our results on the day of, the selection committee—Ross, Coach Jack, and a few other national feder-ation staff members—will take our recent performances into account.

We run through full routines on each apparatus. The Worlds team will be composed of five men, plus two alter-nates, and the Pan-American Games, the next major competi-tion a few weeks later, will consist of another five men and two more alternates. Altogether, there are fourteen spots to fill, and almost double the amount of men competing for them.

If I can put together a good showing today, and then another on the day of selection camp, I have a good shot of pulling away with a spot. The team needs my high potential scores on vault and floor.

I'm about to run through my floor routine when I catch a flash of black out of the corner of my eye. Turning, I'm surprised to see Vivienne in my gym, my sister by her side.

She's wearing dark jeans and a black V-neck T-shirt, her hair pulled back into a simple ponytail. She looks effortlessly casual and put together in a way I envy. I'm not put together even with a *lot* of effort.

Cari waves and gives me a thumbs up. Vivienne checks me out, her gaze lingering on my thighs, exposed by my small shorts, before a slow, smug smile spreads over her face.

"So, that's new," Brody mutters, following my gaze.

"Isn't that the chick from the bar?" Tommy says.

Dylan, the fucker, grins and waves at them.

Coach Jack clears his throat. "Do you need a minute, Gonzales?"

"I'm fine," I mutter, trying to focus.

Brody shoves me forward. "Go say hi to your adoring fans."

"Take a break," Ross announces, making a note on his clipboard. "We'll regroup in a few."

When I catch a glance at Coach's face, he actually looks amused rather than pissed.

I make my way over to where Vivienne and Cari are waiting. A sudden bout of awkwardness overtakes me. What do I do? Do I hug her? Kiss her? Shake her hand?

She surprises me again when she reaches for me and pulls me into a hug.

"Hi," Vivienne says, before she gives me a quick peck on the lips. "I wanted to see you."

"I'm glad you're here," I tell her, and I'm surprised to find that it's one hundred percent true.

Did I expect it? No.

Will there be repercussions for me? Possibly.

Do I want to send her away? Not at all.

Leaning down, I brush my lips against hers again, more firmly this time. She lets out a soft sigh.

"You two are gross," Cari says. But she's grinning, happiness bright in her eyes. I don't think she's upset in the slightest at this development.

Gently, I shove my sister's shoulder, and she laughs.

"My agent wants to talk to you," Vivienne says out of nowhere.

I blink. "What? Why?"

"Do you have an agent?"

"Why would I need one?" I almost laugh. I don't get major social media endorsements. The few I have, I've done the legwork of reaching out to the brands and pitching myself. I don't do it very often because I have trouble believing they're interested in working with me. Usually Brody has to peer pressure me into sending the email.

"Well, she wants to sign you," she says. "A few of my sponsors have reached out. They approve of us."

My stomach drops. Is that something we have to consider, how other people perceive us?

"If there is an us," Vivienne adds quickly.

"There is," I tell her quietly. "I'd like there to be."

"Well, this is one of the bonuses of dating me. Pump It Up Protein wants to do a collaboration." Her smile is strained. "You don't have to. It's totally fine if you're not interested."

"What would it be?" I hold my breath. I almost don't want to know.

"It would be eight posts over eight weeks, we'd get paid five for each post. We'd record videos of ourselves drinking their protein and talking it up." She blows out a breath. "It's a lot. I know. Especially since we—well, it's a lot of pressure."

My mind is spinning. "Can I think about it?"

Vivienne nods. "Yeah. I totally get it. I gave my agent your email, she's sending you some details to look over."

It's a lot of pressure to put on a new relationship. What happens if, on week three, she decides she wants nothing to do with me? All for five hundred dollars a post? Sure, I wouldn't sneeze at an extra four thousand dollars, but not if it means jeopardizing what we have.

"This probably isn't the time." I glance back over at Coach Jack, who's talking to Ross and glancing in our direction.

"Just think it over. Forty thousand dollars could be huge toward paying for vet school."

"Four—" I blink a few times. "I thought you said it was five hundred a post."

Vivienne shakes her head. "Five *thousand* dollars a post. Times eight posts. That means you'd get forty thousand. All you have to do is put up with me for eight weeks." She gives me an awkward, uncomfortable smile.

Forty thousand dollars. That's almost one year of tuition, right there. And all I have to do is make a few social media posts with the woman I'm crazy about??

It takes a couple of seconds for my brain to come back online. When it does, I give her a hard kiss on the lips.

"I don't need money to *put up with you*," I tell her. "I want to be with you. If you want to do this, I'm in, but I don't need this. I don't want to use you. I just want *you*."

A brilliant smile slowly spreads over her face. "You're in?"

"I'm in." I give her a quick kiss. "But now I've got to get back to work."

"Go, go. I can't wait to see you out there."

Jogging back over to the rest of the group, some of the guys are laughing, but the rest are stretching and trying to keep warm. They're actually focused on the goal.

I need to be focused too. I can't get distracted.

Forty thousand dollars. That's, like, life changing. Do I want to gamble Viv's and my fledgling relationship for money?

No. I'll talk to her agent, but I'll make sure there's a clause in there to protect both of us. The protein company probably doesn't actually care about me. They can sub in any guy in my spot. As soon as someone better, more suited for her, comes along, I'm sure they'll be shoving me out the door.

I meant what I said; I don't want to use her to get ahead. If it comes down to it, I'll do whatever it takes to put us first. What we have is infinitely more important than money. I just hope she agrees.

Coach Jack blows his whistle and we get back to work.

And when I nail my floor routine, giving the performance of my life… I start to hope that maybe I can have both—Vivienne *and* a new start at life. I'll do what I have to do.

twenty-one

. . .

Viv

WHEN BIRDIE SPORTSWEAR wanted to host an event for their influencers, I was expecting something low-key. Maybe a yoga day on the Common or brunch at a crunchy hipster café in the trendy part of Cambridge. Am I surprised a holistic-focused company is taking us to dinner at an upscale, Michelin-starred steakhouse? Yes. Am I going to turn it down? No. Hell no.

I get all dolled up in a real bra and a nice dress, my hair and makeup done, and post an enigmatic selfie to Instagram.

The restaurant is in the North End of Boston, a half hour Uber ride from my place in Weymouth. The host of the restaurant looks me up and down with a snooty glare, disapproval written all over his face. I don't know why. I'm adhering to the dress code. I don't have the energy to play his game.

"Can I help you?" he demands.

Lifting my chin, I meet his glare with one of my own. I'm not going to make myself smaller to make him more comfortable.

"I'm here for the Birdie team dinner."

With a put-upon sigh, the host leads me to the back of the restaurant, where a cluster of tables are arranged.

Olivia, Birdie's creative director, stands and greets me with a firm handshake and a wide smile. "Viv. So good to see you again."

"Thanks for thinking of me. I'm so excited for the spring line."

Fashion companies work ahead, so their winter campaign is already shot and getting ready for release, and they're full steam ahead in preparation for the spring launch. Lucky for me, the ad campaign will hit right as my season is starting, boosting my visibility and hopefully driving new fans to the team.

Thank goodness for Alycia. Without her guidance over the last few years, I'd have never put all these pieces together. I'm more of an impulsive, do it right now type person. Sitting on content is such a strain; I just want to release it out into the world right then and there.

Olivia gestures to the table, handing me a name tag. "Come, sit. We're still waiting for a few more."

There are a few people at the table already. I recognize Charlotte Kent, a social media activist, and Courtney Wright, a yoga influencer whose online videos I follow. The rest of them are strangers, but because I was given a dossier with all of their social media handles—they want us all to interact and follow each other—I'm sure their faces will become familiar soon enough.

"Hey, I'm Viv," I say, giving the table a wave. The other women give me a range of polite to cheerful smiles, nods, and waves.

The restaurant's host is coming back toward us, a woman in a wheelchair following him. He removes a chair from the table with an aggrieved sigh.

Through it all, the woman's face is carefully blank, but I can see a fission of tension in her brow at the micro aggression. I can't blame her. I'd probably try to punch the guy if I were her, but that would probably get me into trouble. Assault charges aren't something I want to deal with, even if he deserves it.

"Nicki, I'm glad you made it," Olivia says. "How was your flight?"

"It went well, thank you," Nicki says. She speaks with a British accent and I instantly fall in love with her. "I can't wait to see what you have set for us."

Looking around the table, I see a range of body shapes and sizes. Some of the women are short, others are tall. Some are thin and petite, others are heavier. For a fitness fashion company, I half expected all of their models to be petite, blonde yogis with brilliant smiles and perfect lives where nothing ever goes wrong. Plastic dolls rather than real people.

Seeing them now, real women with real bodies… it makes me feel like maybe I made the right call signing on to this campaign. Sure, Charlotte is blonde and petite—she's a former Team USA gymnast—but she's also been open about her disordered eating struggles.

Hm. I wonder if she knows Tony. That would be a small world.

There's a clamor behind me, and as I turn, my heart starts pounding. Because it's as if I've summoned him. Just seeing him again brings a smile to my face. He's so freaking gorgeous in his black button-up and his dark hair swept back. Butterflies erupt in my belly.

He's not smiling. His eyes are wide and unblinking as he gapes at me. A black apron is tied around his waist.

Shit. Does he work here?

He clears his throat a few times. "Welcome to Quentin's," he finally says. "I'm Tony, I'll be your server tonight. Our specials are—"

Blood rushes in my ears as he speaks. What's he thinking?

Does he think I'm stalking him? I didn't know he worked here. He mentioned working at a fancy restaurant in the North End, and those are a dime a dozen in this neighborhood. We've gone on one date, but we're already talking about public appearances and commitment. Maybe it's too much for him. Fuck, we haven't even had sex yet. What if he changes his mind and I'm too much for him? He might decide I'm more trouble than I'm worth.

Taking a deep breath, I try to recalibrate and calm my racing thoughts. Of course, he doesn't think I'm stalking him. That's an extreme thought to a completely rational behavior. When I get a chance, I'll pull him aside and explain everything. It's going to be fine. It will all work out.

As everyone goes around and places a drink order, I wait for Tony's eyes to land on me. He's calm and collected, distantly professional. He's acting like he doesn't even know me. I can't decide if I want him to acknowledge me or if I want him to pretend like we're strangers.

We're so not strangers. But I also don't want *actual* strangers that I have to work with to know all of my business. My personal life was blasted all over social media without my knowledge or consent. Yes, it's part of what I signed up for with a semi-public career path, and working on brand collaborations like this only makes me more visible. But is it so wrong to want a little bit of privacy for the things that matter most to me?

Olivia launches into a small speech, thanking us all for attending and talking about the company's vision. What started as a yoga apparel company has expanded into a full on athleisure empire. They feature plus-sized women as well as women of color and women with disabilities, and they do it without the models looking like a diversity checkmark. I have to admit, when I first heard about the offer, I was skeptical. At five foot ten and as many muscles as I have, I didn't think I fit their profile.

Hearing her talk now about what the company has in store… I think I believe in their mission.

Growing up, women like me didn't land on the cover of Sports Illustrated. We were told to make ourselves smaller, more palatable for everyone else. We were told our muscles made us unattractive. No matter how physically strong we were, they made us weak.

It's taken a *lot* of work to unlearn all of this. Going to a therapist regularly helped with tackling some of the body dysmorphia and self-esteem issues. A sports psychologist helped me get my head into the game, where it needs to be, instead of up in the clouds worrying about things that don't serve me.

I'm never going to be that bubbly girl who has a bunch of friends and is always in a good mood. There's nothing wrong with her. It's just not me. I thrive on competition and hard work. I'm focused on my rugby career, on performing at the highest levels in my sport, and outside friendships fail when the team has to come first. My resting bitch face tells people to fuck off without me having to do it verbally. Although I do enjoy telling people to fuck off.

The conversation flows easily throughout the meal. Nicki is a hoot, Navaeh has been to a few of our rugby matches, and Blake is adorable. We might not ever be best friends. We might not see each other in person again. But as colleagues and coworkers, I feel comfortable around them in a way I don't usually experience outside of people I know well. Even with other sponsorship opportunities, I typically don't feel so at ease. I feel like I can be myself, grumpy bitch face and all.

Although… I might make an effort to smile in the official campaign photos.

Tony flits around the table, making sure we have everything we need. At one point, he leans between me and Nicki, his fingertips brushing against the back of my neck. I shiver, and he smirks, a satisfied glint to his eye.

Nicki nudges me with a conspiratorial glint in her eyes. "The hot waiter has the hots for you."

"He's my… we're seeing each other," I admit, my face heating. I don't know that I'm ready to announce him as my boyfriend publicly, which is silly if we're going to do a social media campaign together. He's not my dirty little secret.

She lets out a low whistle. "Damn. He's fit."

I nod. "He really is."

Dinner winds down and Olivia and the team give us each a personalized gift bag with two outfits and some accessories. This is on top of all the apparel they're going to send us for promotion and separate from what we'll wear at the photoshoot next month.

It's rare to find a brand that I wholeheartedly believe in their mission and they follow through on their beliefs. Even though I may have had my doubts at the beginning, I am now one hundred percent on board with Birdie. I'm actually looking forward to working with them.

We say our goodbyes and *see you laters*. I delay putting on my coat as long as I possibly can. There's a busboy clearing our table—not Tony. I don't know where he is.

With a sigh, I pull my phone from my pocket. It's not like I don't have a way of contacting him.

To my surprise, I already have a text from him.

I'm working until ten, he's written. *Can I see you tomorrow? Coffee, same place?*

You could come over after your shift, I offer.

That's not a good idea. You have an early morning.

I like that he knows my practice schedule, that he cares about my routine.

We could just sleep.

We won't be sleeping, he texts back immediately. *Tomorrow. Coffee.*

Shaking my head, I can't help my smile as I text back, *it's a date.*

twenty-two

. . .

Tony

I'M AN IDIOT. That's my only conclusion as I knock on Vivienne's door at ten thirty. This is not a good idea. We both have training early tomorrow, plus—

The door swings open. Her eyes widen at the sight of me.

She's wearing a pair of soft cotton pajamas, her long hair tied up in a bun. Her face is free of makeup. It's clear from the look on her face she wasn't expecting me.

This was a bad idea. Maybe I shouldn't have come.

Vivienne reaches for my jacket and yanks me bodily into her apartment. I can hardly breathe before she's shoving me against the door and crashing her lips to mine. Sliding my hand to the back of her neck, I meet her halfway, and the second we connect might be the single best moment of my life. Even better than winning the bronze medal. Want bursts inside of me, flooding my body with anticipation.

Our time together three years ago was brief, a snapshot of time on the precipice of something immense. It hasn't kept me from thinking about it all this time. None of the women I've dated since—the very few and far between—have held a candle to her. Our connection that night, it's the kind of thing people write love songs about.

I've been waiting for her to get on my level. I think she might almost be there.

"I wasn't expecting you," Viv murmurs against my mouth.

Breathing hard, I pull back. "Should I leave?"

I don't want to. It might kill me to walk away right now. But if that's what she needs, who am I to stand in her way? I can't put my wants above her needs.

"Fuck, no." She tugs at my leather jacket, working it off my shoulders and dropping it on the floor.

She goes to kiss me again and I cup her face, running my thumb over her cheek.

"I wanted to see you," I murmur. "I wasn't expecting you, either."

Her coming into my workplace? That wasn't my idea of a good time, having to maintain a specter of professionalism when all I wanted to do was claim her in front of everyone.

More than that, I wasn't expecting her to crash back into my life. I'd lulled myself into a false sense of complacency without her. Now that we've connected again, I don't think I can let her go.

I have a job to do. Three of them, actually. I need to focus on training, on preparing for Worlds. I need…

Her soft brown eyes flicker up to mine, vulnerability shining in their depths.

I need her.

Walking her backward into the apartment, I don't stop to take a look around. Instead, I drop onto her sofa and pull her down onto my lap until she's straddling me, her core directly over my stiff cock. I'm not sure she can feel the hard length of my erection until she shifts and then her eyes go wide, flying up to mine.

Vivienne swallows. "Hi."

"Hi." My face heats, but I won't allow myself to be embarrassed about my body's reaction to her. I don't expect anything from her. If she wants to tell me to get lost, I will. If she wants me to stay the night, I'll wrap her up in my arms and hold her as she drifts off. And if she decides she wants to get naked… well, I'm not about to say no.

Her fingertips trail over my rough cheek. I didn't shave this morning, in too much of a rush to get out the door, so the prickly sensation of the hair beneath her fingers sends pinpricks of delight through me.

"What are we doing?" she asks.

I cock my head. "Like, right this minute, or…?"

"Yeah."

"Well, I'd like to think we're dating," I say lightly. It takes a considerable amount of effort to meet her eyes directly. "Is that what you want?"

"It is," Vivienne says quietly. "I know there are… financial considerations at play."

"There aren't. Not for me."

"The endorsements…"

I shake my head. "Would the money be nice? Yeah. But not at the expense of what we have. If you want me to turn it down so we can be together, I will. What we can have together is more important than money in my bank account."

I can't believe I'm saying it, but I wholeheartedly believe it. Believe in us.

"I'm just worried it's a lot of pressure to put on something new and fragile," she says.

"Right there with you. I don't want you to think I'm using you, trying to take your connections to get ahead," I tell her. "I can get there on my own. This thing with us… it's special."

Vivienne frowns. "I don't think you're using me. I want you to get ahead. I want to help you get there."

"Okay. So I'll meet with your agent," I agree. "But let's not talk about work right now."

A smile curves across her lips. "Oh? What would you like

to talk about?" She shifts over my hard, aching cock, her eyes fluttering.

Kissing her jaw, I work my way down the column of her neck, licking and sucking her skin. She smells like strawberries and tastes even better.

"How about politics? Current events?" I suck on the spot below her ear, and just like I remember, she gasps and arches against me. "The state of the economy?"

She pulls back. "Or what if we talk about getting naked?"

"You only want me for my body," I tease, but there's a shred of truth to my fears. What if this is only physical for her? I can't separate sex from emotions. They're too intertwined for me.

When it comes to her, I'm hopelessly devoted.

"I mean, it's nice," Vivienne says, running her hand over my chest. "I like other things about you too."

"Oh yeah? Like what?" Is it obvious I'm fishing for compliments?

"Like, you're driven and ambitious. You're working hard for your goals. That's sexy," she says. Her hands curve around the back of my neck. "You have a huge heart. You act like a grumpy bear, but you care deeply about your friends and family, even if you'd try to deny it," she says, her eyes narrowing. And I have to laugh, because she's right on the money there. "The way you held that tiny kitten…"

"Shadow. I adopted her," I admit.

She bites her lip, and gently I pull it from between her teeth, rubbing the pad of my thumb over the indentations.

"When I saw you take her home on your motorcycle…" She mimes fanning herself.

I grin. "Yeah?"

"Almost as hot as when you took me on your bike."

"We can do that again, anytime you want," I offer.

Vivienne's smile fades. Her face creases with sadness. "You can't do that."

"Do what?"

"Make promises you don't intend to keep."

"What makes you think I don't intend to keep them?"

"I'm… a lot." She looks away.

Taking her chin between my fingers, I wait until she looks back at me. Uncertainty shines in her eyes.

I don't think she lets people in. She keeps up a front, pretending like everything is okay, while inside she's a mess of emotions she never lets anyone see.

"I want to keep you," I tell her. I'll keep telling her until she believes me. "For as long as you'll have me."

She swallows heavily. "You'll change your mind."

"I won't."

"Everyone else does."

"I'm not everyone else." I brush my fingers over her cheek. "You're worth fighting for, putting in the hard work. *You're worth it.*"

I see the moment it finally clicks for her. It's like a bomb detonated inside her brain and she's left at the site of the blast, debris floating around her. We can work on that. We can tackle this—together.

Her mouth crashes onto mine. Surging forward, I slide my hand into her hair and meet her lips with my own, licking into her mouth. Our teeth clack in our mutual eagerness and she laughs against my lips.

Pulling back slightly, Vivienne reaches for the hem of her sleep shirt. My hands land on her strong hips, not pressuring her either way. If she wants to get naked, I'm all for it. If she decides she'd like to end the night here, I won't fight her on it. It's been an emotionally charged night. I won't hold it against her if she needs time to decompress.

She whips her T-shirt over her head, leaving her top half bare to me. My eyes roll back in my head and I think I'm drooling.

Vivienne is a solid wall of muscle and strength. Her shoulders are rock solid, her biceps toned and sleek. Her strong waist and the flare of her hips are just as attractive to me as her obvious dedication to her sport.

Her strength is sexy.

Moving my hands to cup her breasts, they're the perfect handful. The tight buds of her nipples pebble against my calloused palms.

"I think I'm dead," I admit quietly.

She cocks her head.

"I've died and gone to heaven."

Vivienne bursts into laughter. "You're ridiculous."

"Only for you." I kiss her, hard, tugging her more firmly onto my lap until there's nothing between us except a few scraps of fabric.

She scrambles for my shirt, undoing the first few buttons before she lets out a grunt of frustration and rips the thing off me. I'm wearing a T-shirt underneath it, and as I help take it off, I'm treated to the sight of her sliding her hand into her sleep shorts.

My cock jerks in my pants, and I know she can feel it because her eyes widen before she shifts on top of me, shamelessly grinding on top of me.

Maneuvering her off me, I lay her out on the couch and reach for the waistband of her shorts. She helps me get them off, lifting her hips, and I fling the fabric away. It lands somewhere behind me. I don't care right now. She's fully nude, her strong, toned body on display for me.

I'm going to be good. This is about *her*.

My cock is aching, throbbing, and as I reach down to squeeze myself firmly, she reaches for the button on my pants.

Fuck it.

Working my pants off my hips, I let them drop, and then crawl onto the couch, on top of her. I'm still wearing my boxers. That's my line in the sand. If she wants more, she'll have to make the next move. I won't pressure her into going farther than she's comfortable. If she changes her mind and doesn't want to do this, I might die.

It would be worth it.

We collide in a frantic crash of lips and tongues. I can't stop touching her, cataloguing her smooth skin and sexy muscles. Her bare skin pressed to mine is doing funny things to my heart rate.

Vivienne wraps her legs around my waist, bringing us into direct, intimate contact. The heat of her cunt against my fabric-covered cock makes me jerk and twitch against her. Giving an experimental roll of my hips, I grind up into her core and she shudders beneath me. The friction on my cock feels…

Her hands rove over my shoulders, my arms, my back, like she can't get enough of me, either. When I suck on that spot just beneath her ear, her nails rake down my back, digging into my lats. The little pricks of pain send even more blood rushing to my cock, making me even harder. I don't think I've ever been this insanely turned on before.

She's rocking her hips, grinding her bare pussy onto my cock. The slick heat of her cunt leaves a wet mess on my boxers. I'll wear her brand like a badge of honor. Her hand slides into my hair, guiding my mouth back to hers. Relentless, she takes what she needs, using me for her pleasure. I'll happily be her toy to use as she'd like whenever she wants.

She nips at my lips. It's hard to concentrate on kissing her breathless when her slick pussy heats me to my core.

Breathing hard, Vivienne's mouth opens in a silent scream. Her entire body goes tense as her hips jerk against mine. It takes everything in me not to lose my rhythm, giving her exactly what she needs as she twitches and trembles beneath me. Her fingernails dig into my skin almost to the point of pain, raking a line down my back.

She sags against the couch, a sated, satisfied smile lighting her face. She finally looks relaxed. Happy.

And that's what does it for me. Burying my face in her neck, breathing her in, I let myself go. It only takes a few swivels of my hips against hers before I seize above her, my orgasm hitting me like a freight train. My release floods my boxers, leaving me wet and sticky in the mess.

Collapsing on top of her, it takes everything in me to hold my weight off her. But Vivienne wraps her arms firmly around me and tugs me down until I'm resting on top of her, my weight pinning her onto the sofa.

"Mm." She runs her hand lazing through my hair. "That was nice."

I pull back to meet her gaze. "Yeah?"

Viv nods, her eyes half-mast like she can hardly keep them open. "Yeah. We're going to have to do that again."

"Anytime you'd like." Kissing her softly, I cup her cheek, marveling at her smooth softness.

A warm burst of happiness floods through me, lighting me from my head to my toes.

Slowly maneuvering off her, I work my way to standing and wince at the mess in my boxers. That'll be fun to deal with later.

For now, I help her up and then lift her into my arms. Vivienne lets out a giggle when I toss her over my shoulder, my hand sliding over the curve of her ass and squeezing before I return it to her back.

I stride into her bedroom, laying her out on the unmade bed. Pulling the covers over her, I press a soft kiss to her forehead.

She blinks up at me through sleepy eyes. "You're not staying?"

"Do you want me to?"

"I do." Some of that earlier vulnerability is in her expression again. "Stay with me."

Cupping her cheek, I run my thumb over the curve of her smile. "Okay. I will. Let me clean up first."

Vivienne nods, shifting in the bed to watch as I navigate the small apartment to figure out where her bathroom is. Leaving the soiled boxers, I do the world's fastest clean-up job and return to her, crawling naked into her bed and pulling her into my arms like it's the most natural thing in the world.

Because it is.

She turns in the circle of my arms, wrapping her arm around my waist and resting her head on my chest. "Good night," she says around a yawn.

Hiding a smile, I kiss the top of her head. "Sleep well."

With her in my arms, I know I will.

twenty-three

• • •

Viv

I'M IN TROUBLE. *Big* trouble.

Waking up in Tony's arms has quickly become my favorite thing. It's been a week since our first sleepover and he's spent the night four more times. He comes over after his shift at the steakhouse, fucks me senseless, then pulls me into his arms and holds me until I fall asleep.

The worst part? Every morning, I expect him to be long gone, just like our first time together.

The best part? Every morning, he's right there beside me, holding me close.

No matter how many times he says he'll be beside me, I can't help expecting for him to leave and leave me disappointed again. How am I supposed to trust that he means it this time?

Slowly, I pull myself from his arms and slide out of the bed. After I pull on one of his T-shirts and make a quick stop to brush my teeth, I turn on the coffeemaker and start pulling out supplies for breakfast. He has training this morning, same as I do. They're supposed to announce the Worlds team any day now. I think I'm more anxious about the team selection than he is. I want him to be picked. I want him to succeed at the highest echelon of his sport.

The coffeemaker whirs and drips slowly, flooding the apartment with the heavenly aroma of freshly brewed coffee. Tony emerges from my bedroom as I'm dicing up some fruit, his hair a mess. His eyes droop sleepily as he approaches, tugging me into his arms and pressing a soft kiss to my lips. He tastes minty fresh, the spicy sandalwood of his soap enveloping me. I can't get enough as I bury my face in his neck and inhale, rubbing my cheek against his skin like a cat.

"Good morning," he says, his voice rough and sleep-hoarse. "Did you sleep well?"

"Mm. You tired me out." He ate me out on the sofa for what felt like hours before flipping me onto my hands and knees and fucking me until I screamed. I've already gotten a text from my downstairs neighbor congratulating me on finding a new boyfriend and asking that we keep it down.

Tony wears a self-satisfied smile as I continue slicing strawberries. He swipes one from the cutting board and I bare my teeth at him. His laugh and cheeky grin warm me to my core.

"I've got to run," he says.

"You want a shake?" I've got about fifty varieties of protein powder in my cupboard, courtesy of Pump It Up Protein. He still hasn't signed the contract with them—or with Alycia for representation. I'm not sure what the holdup is, but I don't want to pressure him.

"Nah. I'll make one at home. I've got to check on Shadow."

"Is she okay?"

He pauses. "I hope so. Cari is looking after her. She has some separation anxiety, but I'm worried my being gone all the time isn't helping. Taking her back and forth to the shelter stresses her out, but I don't want to leave her alone all day long, either. I wasn't expecting to fall into a relationship immediately after adopting her."

"Do you want to bring her here?" I don't know the first thing about kitty-proofing my place, but for him, I'll gladly do it.

Tony shakes his head. "At my place, there's a better chance of one of the three of us being able to look after her. We're in and out all day. I don't want to chain you down."

"Hey, I might like that," I tease.

Laughing, he swipes another strawberry from the board, this time bringing it to my lips. I suck it into my mouth, my tongue flicking against his fingertips in the process. His breath hitches and his pupils expand.

"You'd be up for that?"

Being chained up? I've never considered it before. I've never really experimented with the kink scene. As much as I like reading about it in books, I've never found a guy I trusted enough to let loose with.

I trust Tony. It terrifies me how much I trust him. But I know he's the type of guy to treat me right, to be mindful of my limits and check on me.

"I'm up for anything once." I shrug. "I reserve the right not to enjoy it."

"If you don't like it, we don't have to…"

"We'll never know unless we try." Turning in the circle of his arms, I wrap mine around his neck. "What else are you into? Any secret fantasies I should be aware of?"

His face goes pink. "Nope. Nothing."

Oh, he's *definitely* hiding something. I bet it's dirty. I can't wait.

I can't hide my smile as I kiss him. "So you don't want to go to a sex shop together?"

Tony chokes.

"We can look into toys we can use on each other. Maybe some flavored lube?"

"Whatever you want," he says, his voice strangled.

"Does talking about sex make you uncomfortable?" I tilt my head as I study him. With how enthusiastic he's been thus far, I didn't peg him as a prude.

Mm. Pegging. I'd love to peg *him*. I've never done it before, but like they say, there's a first time for everything.

"I didn't think you'd be interested in toys," he says. "Most women…" He winces, as if he's recognizing that bring up whatever past he has with whoever they were might not be what I want to hear.

I have a past. So does he. I don't care about his history or who he's been with as long as he's not with anyone else now.

"I'm not them. Our sex life is between us and nobody else." Running my hand through his hair, he arches into my touch. "If you don't want to play with toys, we don't have to. But it could be fun."

He swallows loudly, his Adam's apple bobbing in his throat. Fuck. Why is that so hot?

"Maybe… we can look online? Especially not with the recent media attention, I don't know that I'm ready to step foot in a store."

"It's a date." I peck him on the lips.

He doesn't let me get far, kissing me again. His tongue licks into my mouth, teasing mine. He tastes like strawberries with an undercurrent of his unique flavor. I can't get enough of him.

His phone alarm slices through the air, puncturing the moment. With a sigh, he slips away, giving me one last kiss before he pulls back. I watch the muscles in his bare back flex as he retreats to my bedroom, returning a few moments later dressed in his clothes. If I had it my way, he'd be naked all the time.

"I'm at the shelter this afternoon," he says, then stops.

I wait for him to continue. He doesn't.

"Do you want to do something after?" I ask.

He swallows. "Maybe… you could come over to my place? My siblings will be home, Al doesn't have a game and Cari's always there, but maybe…"

"I'd love to."

I want his siblings to like me. I'm fairly certain Cari does, she can't stop beaming at me every chance she gets, and I think I won Al over that night at the bar. But being a friendly acquaintance in public is different from being their brother's girlfriend. If we keep hiding away in my apartment and never going out or being around other people, we run the risk of this imploding before it ever really gets started.

It's easy to put on a mask and pretend. It's harder to be real with people watching. If this isn't going to work out, if I'm too much for him, I'd rather find out sooner rather than later.

He says he's not going anywhere. He says I'm worth it. But what if he changes his mind? I want to trust him, I really do. I just don't know how to.

twenty-four

. . .

Tony

THIS IS IT. Do or die.

Standing at the top of the ramp, I stare at the vault sixty feet away. I can do this. I've been training like crazy for the past few months, getting ready for this. It all comes down to this one, singular moment.

Hopping into a run, I sprint down the ramp toward the table. After a round-off onto the springboard and a back handspring onto the table, I stretch my body into the layout position as I twist three and a half times. Focusing on my breathing, I keep my eyes on my spot, letting physics do its thing while I twist.

The landing comes out of nowhere. I'm not prepared for my feet to crash into the mat. I brace my knees and dig my toes in, sticking the landing by the skin of my teeth.

I did it. I landed the vault.

Cheers go up from my teammates on the sidelines. I glance over at them, genuine happiness on their faces as they cheer for me.

Yes, we're competing against each other. They're picking the teams for the next two major competitions. While I wouldn't say boo to a spot on the Pan-American Games team, we all want one of the coveted World Championships team positions.

There are only five spots on the Worlds team plus two alternates and there are twenty-four guys competing. All the guys on the national team have come to Boston for this selection camp, plus a few college gymnasts who were invited for consideration. The elite gymnastics world is a small, tightly knit community, and at the end of the day, we want Team USA to do well. We want *each other* to do well.

Brody slaps my back as I walk past. "Nice one," he says, handing me my water bottle.

"Thanks." I'm in the middle of the vault rotation, with a few more guys to compete after me. I tear the tape from my wrists and prepare to re-wrap them. Each apparatus requires a different level of support and preparation.

There are six apparatuses in men's gymnastics compared to four in women's gymnastics. For men, we compete in the vault and floor exercise, same as the women, plus pommel horse, still rings, parallel bars, and horizontal bar. I'm not the best at rings or either of the two bars events, I can hold my own, and I'm decent at pommel horse. I can contribute decent routines for a team score.

Where I shine is on the floor and the vault. My legs are more powerful than my arms. Tumbling has always come more naturally to me than the strength exercises.

We rotate through our events, putting on a show for the selection committee. Ross, the national team's coordinator, gets the final say with input from Coach Jack and a handful of other Team USA executives.

When we're done with all six rotations, we break for lunch in the cafeteria as they deliberate our fates. Whereas normally I'd be ravenous, right now I can't eat.

I've been glib about wanting a spot on the team. I want it. I want it bad. This is my last chance to make my mark on the world of gymnastics. Sure, I've been to two World Championships, bringing home a few silver and bronze medals. Sure, I'm an Olympic bronze medalist, helping to earn the first team medal for my country since 2008. I'm internationally ranked and well-respected among my peers.

But as much as I'm ready to be done with the world of gymnastics, to move on to the next stage of my life and hopefully go to vet school... I'm not ready to be done with it, either.

Making the Olympics next summer is a pipe dream. A lot will depend on how I do throughout the rest of this competition season. If I make the Worlds team, I might be able to find the push to compete for a spot on the Olympic team.

But if I don't make this team... that's it. I'll compete the rest of this season, I'll still give it my best, but I'm prepared to walk away.

It's not that I want to be done. I'm one back injury away from possible permanent damage. My knees always ache. My wrists are shot. I want to be able to grow old and still have a functioning body, I want to be able to walk and run and bend down. Take care of my patients.

Maybe one day, run around after some kids. Maybe not. I haven't decided whether I want kids, it's too far in the future for me to think about. I'd be fine with nieces and nephews. I know I want animals in my home. That's enough for me, at least for right now.

But first: Worlds. Maybe the Olympics. Then vet school. The rest can all be figured out later.

Ross calls us all into the small conference room. The team staff are all gathered around the back of the room, Coach Jack with an inscrutable expression on his face. I don't think that's good. Shouldn't he be happy? They've decided on the team!

A rush of nerves runs through me as I take a seat at the conference table. Brody and Dylan, on either side of me, each give me fist bumps. My deep inhalation rattles through my chest as I try to calm my racing heart.

"We've put a lot of thought into the teams," Ross says. "We've tried to find a balance between what the team needs and rewarding your hard work and consistency." He goes on about what an honor it is to wear the country's badge on our chest and how we've made Team USA proud, all the flattery with none of the fanfare.

"For the Pan-American Games," Coach Jack says, "We've got Brayden, Connor, Paul, Davis, and Joseph. Alternates will be Max and Will."

My stomach drops. I'm not named to the team.

Well… I didn't want to go to the Pan-American Games. I want to go to Worlds.

There's still a chance. It's not over yet.

Ross takes over. "For World Championships, the team will be Brody, Tommy, Dylan, Steve, and Tony. Alternates are—"

Blood rushes through my veins so fast it makes me dizzy. I can hardly breathe.

I did it.

I have one more shot. One more chance. One more opportunity.

I'm sure as fuck not going to waste it.

Brody turns to me, giving me a fist bump. "We did it," he says, a happy smile on his face.

"We've got this."

"We should go out tonight," Dylan says. Steve lives in Colorado, training at a facility out there. He leaves in the morning. The two alternates, Alex and Doug, leave the day after. They're both still in college.

"Unless you've got plans with your girl?" Tommy raises his eyebrows at me.

It's no secret that Vivienne and I are together. Between the kisses being caught on social media, which the guys ribbed me about endlessly, and the smiles on my face the last few days at training, it's been fairly obvious that I'm seeing someone new.

I'd shout it from the rooftops if I didn't value my privacy. Just because I'm a semi-public athlete doesn't mean I can't have a private, personal life too.

"We've got plans," I say simply, and he smirks at me.

The coaches release us for the day. It's a rare break before my shift at the shelter this afternoon, so I swing by the grocery store for some supplies for dinner. There will be four of us in the same room for the first time. I can't wait for her to meet my siblings properly, to get to know them. She's my partner, but they're my family. They have to get along.

Vivienne is my first call. She doesn't answer—I know she's at training—so I leave her a quick voicemail telling her we're celebrating tonight.

Alycia is my second.

"I'll do it. I'll sign," I tell her.

"Great," my new agent says. "Let's get started."

twenty-five

. . .

Viv

MY STOMACH FLUTTERS with nerves as I approach the Mattapan townhouse. I haven't been back here since the day I found out about Tony and my past connection. Although I know Tony and I are solid now, although Cari and I get along and I liked Al the one time I met him, I can't help being nervous. If my siblings didn't like my partner, I'd listen to their opinions why. I'd at least hear them out.

If Cari and Al don't like me with Tony…

I can't even think about it. Yes, we're new, and I'm already in over my head, but I can't picture doing this without him. In such a short amount of time, he's brought so much happiness into my life, I don't know what to do with myself.

The front door swings open without my having rung the bell. Cari beams at me.

"You going to stay out here all night?" she teases.

Forcing a smile onto my face, I summon all of my bravery. "Maybe."

My teammate laughs, shaking her head. "Come on in."

The house looks the same as it does before, but where I was too panicked to notice the little details, now I drink them in. There are photos on the mantel and on the wall. A few throw pillows and a soft-looking knit blanket. A basket full of cat toys.

Shadow, the little black kitten, isn't so little anymore. She comes running toward me, then stops just in front of me, staring up at me. I stare down at her, meeting her eyes. After a moment, the cat bats at my leg with her paw and then darts off.

Through the small kitchen, I can see Tony at the stove, sauteing something that smells fantastic. I watch his back muscles flex through his T-shirt as he expertly controls three different pans. I think I might drool.

"Damn, girl," Cari says, shaking her head. "You've got it bad."

"Yeah, I do." I'm not ashamed of how much I care for him.

Does it scare me? Yes.

Am I hiding it? No. Hell no.

There's a rumble on the stairs and then Al appears in a T-shirt and sweatpants, his hair wet. He stops short at the sight of me.

"Viv. Hey. Great to see you again." Before I know what's happening, he tugs me into a light hug.

There's a clatter in the kitchen and I turn to see Tony watching us, glaring in our direction.

"I don't think he likes this very much," Al teases, slinging his arm around my shoulder.

Tony's eyes meet mine and his hard glare softens. I'm not about the jealousy game. I never want him to question exactly how I feel about him.

Shrugging off Al's arm, I make my way into the kitchen, wrapping my arms around Tony's waist from behind. He leans back into me, turning his head so he can kiss me.

"Hey." His voice rumbles through me. "You made it."

"Wouldn't miss it for the world." I rest my head on his shoulder. "Whatcha making?"

"Chicken fajitas." His shoulder lifts beneath my chin as he stirs the peppers and onions.

"Smells good." I breathe him in, his familiar, spicy scent undercut by fragrant garlic and cumin.

"Can I get you a drink?"

"I'm good for now, thanks." I'm content to watch him cook, but it's not really safe to cling to him like a barnacle, so I move to the kitchen barstools.

Cari slides onto the stool beside mine. We had a good practice today. The team is really gelling and we're starting to nail the plays. We're still in the reconditioning period, where everyone is getting used to the intense physicality of the sport again. Not all of us had summer off for the Sevens season, so the few of us who did compete are still in pretty decent shape, but it takes a while to get back into the groove of things.

Our first match isn't until early February. We've got plenty of time to get dialed in.

Al plops down at the kitchen table, looking at his phone. He makes a surprised noise.

"What's wrong?" Cari asks her brother.

"My agent just got an offer from Pump It Up Protein," Al says slowly. His eyes flit to mine, then Tony's. "He's asking if you have an agent, Car."

"Not yet. I don't think I need one."

She had a couple of Name, Image, and Likeness deals in college, but she managed them on her own. I don't think she's done any sort of endorsement since graduating last spring.

Al laughs. "Well, you better sign, quick. They want to do a Gonzales family promotion campaign."

Tony whips his head around. "They want to do what?"

"They're highlighting the fact that all three of us are professional athletes." Al shakes his head. "They specifically mentioned your promotion with them."

"Did you sign the contract?" I ask my boyfriend, who nods.

"When I made the team this morning, I called Alycia and she sent over the contract. We're all set."

My smile stretches from ear to ear. As much as I'm happy about the endorsement campaign for my own selfish reasons, I'm happy for him too. I want him to receive the recognition he so clearly deserves for how hard he works.

"This could be life changing for you guys. I know the money is only part of it, the exposure opportunities are huge. This is only the start." I wholeheartedly believe that. This could bring them to a whole new level. Alycia is a bulldog and will reach out to everyone to help get him opportunities. He can earn enough to pay for vet school.

"Do you do campaigns with your brothers?" Cari asks me.

"I did one with the twins for Pump It Up and I did another with Janine for an airline. She's the swimmer," I explain. "We did a few campaigns before the last Olympics, since we were both there. The press loved the sisters competing together, not against each other storyline."

Janine did *not* have a good Olympic experience. She didn't qualify for her best event, and the one she did qualify for, she didn't win any medals. She likes to say just getting there was an accomplishment, and it is, but I know she's on the quest for redemption. She's ready to prove all the doubters wrong. I couldn't be more ready to watch her dominate her field.

Al hums. "So you think we should do it?"

I shrug. "It's up to the three of you. Pump It Up is a brand I actually believe in. They pay well, they treat me right, and I genuinely like the product."

"She has, like, seventy different protein powders from them," Tony comments from the stove.

I smile. It's not that many. "It's not a hardship to work with them."

"My agent *has* been trying to work on some new endorsement opportunities…" Al says.

"Alycia—that's my new agent—she mentioned that she has a whole list of ideas for the three of us," Tony says.

My eyebrows go up. "Really? That's so cool!"

"But only if all three of us are on board." His eyes flick toward Cari. "I'd understand if you're not interested. It's a lot. You get to live a relatively private life right now. That might change."

"I can do it," she says with all the optimism and positivity of someone who has no idea the kind of power she wields. "I want girls to see women succeeding in sports. If I can do my part to show the world that women are just as strong and capable as men, I will."

"So you're in?" Al glances at me, then Tony.

He shrugs. "If you guys both want to do it, sure. I don't think they want me though. People don't care about gymnastics."

"They do," Al says firmly. "It's all of us or none of us."

Tony sighs. "Then yes. Let's do it."

"This will be great," Al says, typing on his phone. He grins over at me. "You're pushing him out of his comfort zone. I like it."

"Not pushing," I correct. "Just… supporting."

Tony gives me a soft smile before turning back to the stove. He bustles around the small kitchen, moving the food to serving platters. There's barely enough room for one person to move around, much less two, so I don't offer to help, even though I want to. I don't like being waited on.

The small table is set for four already, and as Tony brings the food to the table, Cari gets up and heads to the fridge.

"Can I get you anything to drink?" she asks me.

"Water would be great, thanks." I catch Tony's arm on his way past me and he curls his arm around me, leaning into me as much as I'm leaning on him. He presses a soft kiss on the top of my head before releasing me.

These stolen moments, a quick snuggle or a sweet display

of affection, mean the world to me. With every one, I'm slowly starting to drop my guard. I'm finally starting to believe him when he says he's not going anywhere.

As we sit at the table, Tony sets his hand on my leg. We haven't shared a lot of sit-down meals together. He typically arrives at my apartment after his restaurant shift and isn't hungry for food, only for my pussy. When we have breakfast after a sleepover, we're usually standing at my kitchen island before we run out the door for training.

This is nice.

And as Al and Cari talk around us, it's nice being with them too. I don't see my siblings very often, we're all spread out across the country, so it's nice to feel like part of a family unit.

"You know," Al says slowly, and I force my attention back to the conversation. "We're playing Colorado next month."

"My brother plays for Colorado."

He grins. "I know. What's the chance we can get together with him?"

I blink. "You want to get together with my brother?"

"Yeah. Gotta see if he approves of this *pendejo*." Al nods toward Tony. "I can't wait to see the big brother inquisition."

"Chuck is younger than me." I focus on that part. My hand falls to Tony's leg and I squeeze. "There will be no inquisition. I'm happy, so he'll be happy for me."

"I can handle it," Tony says through a scowl. "He can interrogate me all he wants. He won't scare me away."

My heart gives a loud thump and my throat gets choked up as I lean over to kiss him. He kisses me softly, cupping my cheek.

Across the table, Al gags. "We get it, you're in love and shit," he says. "We don't want to see it."

Tony withdraws, flipping his middle finger at his brother. "Fuck off," he growls, but there's no heat in his voice.

Cari grins, shaking her head. "They're cute. Leave them alone."

When Al opens his mouth, she pinches his arm. And from the wince on his face, I'm guessing it hurts. Dutifully, he shuts up and focuses on his dinner.

The chicken fajitas are great. Tony also made a pot of brown rice, black beans, and an extra platter of veggies. There is a little dish of homemade pico de gallo, freshly sliced avocado, diced onions, cilantro, and fresh limes. A folded kitchen towel holds warm corn tortillas.

"I didn't know you could cook," I comment to Tony. "This is delicious."

He gives me a shy smile. "Gotta eat."

"You're going to have to cook for me more often," I tease.

His face goes pink, and he nods. "If you want me to."

I cook because I have to, not because I enjoy it. Food is fuel. It's not a hobby for me.

"I do." Squeezing his leg again, I return my attention to the fantastic meal he prepared. I can taste the love and care he put into it.

After dinner, Al puts away the leftovers and Cari loads the dishwasher. I offer to help, but they all turn me down. Tony tugs me onto the sofa and pulls me into his arms. Shadow, his little kitten, jumps into his lap and starts kneading his thighs. I try to hide my flinch, and when the kitten doesn't make any moves to scratch or bite me, I slowly start to relax. She's not a murder kitty like the one we had growing up. I don't have to be scared of her.

"Want to watch a movie?" he asks, reaching for the remote.

"Sure. Whatever you want." I rest my head on his shoulder, breathing him in.

Shadow purrs and I chance a slow stroke of the top of her head. She leans into the contact, her motor going.

Tony and I haven't had a lot of time to just hang out,

clothes on. I'm a little relieved to realize I still like him with his clothes on. It's more than physical chemistry. There's something here.

And from the way he's glancing at me out of the corner of his eye, hiding his smile, I think he's feeling it too.

Al and Cari join us for the movie, an action-adventure film with lots of explosions and terribly misogynistic comments, where the female character is clearly meant to be a sex symbol and not an actually fleshed out person.

After one particularly heinous scene, Tony winces. "I did *not* know the movie would be like this. I regret everything."

"We can turn it off," Al says. "The Triumph are playing."

So we turn on the basketball game, and as I settle back against Tony, it turns into a much nicer evening.

At ten, Cari stretches and gives a fake yawn. "Okay, I'm out," she says, giving me a pointed look.

Oh. Does she want me to go home? Am I not supposed to stay?

"I've got earplugs and a white noise machine ready," she goes on. "But I'd really rather not hear any noises, if you know what I mean."

My face heats. *Fuck.* She's not kicking me out; she's expecting me to stay the night with her brother. Somehow, that's even worse.

"We'll keep it down," Tony says, his entire body coiled and tense. "Good night."

twenty-six

. . .

Tony

I LEAD Viv up to my bedroom. Since I took over the master when my parents moved out, I have my own private bathroom and a decent amount of space. I look over the room with a critical eye, wondering what she thinks. I'm not really much for decorating.

The walls are bare, no posters, no pictures. There's a bed I put fresh sheets on this afternoon, a dresser, two nightstands, and an armchair in the corner. Shadow has a small bed and a basket of toys next to her tower. I've picked up the things I'd strewn about the room, but it still feels cluttered. Or maybe that's just my imagination.

Viv looks around the room curiously. Folding my arms over my chest, I wait for her opinion.

"Where's Shadow?" she asks.

I wasn't expecting that.

"She sleeps in Cari's room lately."

"Because you've been staying with me." It's not a question.

I shrug. "I didn't ask her to. She likes her."

Viv bites her lip, and I step closer to her, setting my hands on her hips.

"What's wrong?"

"Is it bad that I'm kind of glad she's not sleeping in here?" Her face goes pink. "I don't know that I'd be able to relax if she was in the room when we're naked."

A bolt of heat runs through me. "Oh? We're getting naked?" I try to play it cool.

She pins me with a flat look. "If you think I'm going to lay in this bed beside you all night without touching you, you have another think coming."

Shaking my head, I hide my smile by pulling her close for a kiss. She winds her arms around my neck, her chest pressed to mine so close she can probably feel my heart pounding for her.

Viv yields for me, melting into me. Slowly, I walk her toward the bed until it hits the back of her legs. To my surprise, she sits on the edge and then looks up at me, her dark eyes bright.

I grab the back of my T-shirt, pulling it up and off. It lands somewhere behind me. Her hands reach for the waistband of my joggers. My hard cock slaps up against my abs, leaving a smear of pre-cum on my skin. I shiver at the sensation.

When she wraps her hand around my cock, giving me a slow stroke, I nearly combust. She smirks up at me, a pleased look on her face.

And then she leans forward, wrapping her lips around me. She draws me into the tight heat of her mouth, her tongue playing with the sensitive spot beneath the head of my cock. I bite down on my knuckles to smother my groan.

Vivienne grabs my other hand, setting in on the back of her head. I thread my fingers through her hair, gripping the strands as she draws back and then takes me deeper, her cheeks hollowing as she sucks.

My hips punch forward involuntarily and she lets out a soft sound. Immediately, I pull back to give her space to breathe, but she doesn't let me. She takes me deeper, her hand moving to my ass and pulling me toward her.

Her other hand strokes the parts of me that won't fit in her mouth. Her tight grip feels incredible. I think I could come just from this. But I don't want the night to be over just yet.

My hand in her hair, I pull her head back until she draws off. She's breathing hard, her face pink. My cock is wet with her saliva and I immediately regret leaving the perfect heat of her mouth.

Except her pleasure comes first. Every time. That's a nonnegotiable for me.

As I reach for the hem of her shirt, she helps me lift it off. She's wearing a soft, dark green bra and leggings. I don't waste time in helping her out of them. They land somewhere on the floor behind me, as do her lacy boy short-style panties.

When she's naked in my bed, staring up at me with want in her eyes, it's like all my dreams have come true. Fuck chasing a gold medal at Worlds. Fuck going back to the Olympics. *This* is what I want. This is what's important.

I cover her body with mine. She wraps her arms around me, pulling me further into her. My cockhead nudges her entrance, her hot, slick cunt on my skin making my eyes roll back in my head. I rock my hips into hers, not trying to enter her, slipping and sliding against her slick skin. Vivienne lets out a soft moan, throwing her head back.

Well, don't mind if I do. Kissing down the column of her throat, I taste her skin, sucking on that sensitive spot where her neck meets her shoulder.

I make my way down the bed, paying good attention to her breasts. They're the perfect handful, the pointed nubs begging to be tugged and licked and sucked. I make sure to devote equal attention to both, my hands and mouth busy. Her fingers card through my hair, holding me tight to her.

Her soft pants and breathy moans drive me absolutely crazy. I kiss my way down her belly to her core, opening her for me. She helps by spreading her legs wider. I draw one leg over my shoulder, then the other, before I dive in and taste her.

As much as I love being inside her, I think I could do this for the rest of my life and die happy. Don't get me wrong, the physicality of sex and the emotional connection we share are toe-curling good. Bringing her pleasure? It makes everything better for me when she's having a good time and enjoying herself. Her happiness is my highest priority at all times, in bed and out of it.

Vivienne's heels dig into my back, her hands in my hair, as her face rides my mouth. She isn't shy about taking what she needs from me. Slipping two fingers inside her, I search for that spot that drives her crazy.

When I find it, she lets out a loud, long groan, her head tipped back. She fists my hair, pulling at the strands almost to the point of pain. My cock jerks and leaks against the comforter.

But I don't let up. I give her what she needs, again and again. And when she finally breaks, her walls fluttering around my fingers and drenching my hand, I've never seen anything so beautiful.

She reaches for me, pulling me by the shoulders until we're face to face. Without hesitation, she kisses me, no doubt tasting herself on my lips. She deepens the kiss, our tongues tangling, our breaths commingling until we're one soul in two bodies, forever intertwined.

Vivienne breaks the kiss, panting hard. "Please tell me you have a condom," she says. Her fingertips trail down my torso, dipping into the divots of my abs, stopping just above my cock.

Rolling over, I dig in the nightstand for the brand new box I bought the other day. She wraps her body around mine, spooning me from behind. I have to admit, I like the feeling of her body pressed to mine like this. Her hand slides up my thigh to cup my balls, rolling them in her palm.

I tear a condom off the strip and turn back to her. She gives me a quick kiss before she grabs the condom from me, ripping it open and rolling the latex down my length, giving me a firm stroke. I expect her to settle against the bed, so I'm surprised when she grabs me by the shoulders and tosses me onto the bed.

My cock jerks. I didn't think I'd be interested in being tossed around like a rag doll, but when Viv does it… yes. Please. Give me more. We're roughly the same size, though I outweigh her by a good thirty pounds of muscle. She uses her strength and athleticism to manhandle me the way she wants me: on my back, with her straddling me.

She rises up on her haunches and positions the head of my cock at her entrance. Where I expect her to go slowly, she drives her hips down and slides down my length in one fluid motion.

A stuttered groan pulls from my throat. Her tight, wet heat surrounds my cock, engulfing me. My eyes roll back in my head and it takes everything in me to breathe through it without erupting.

Viv squeezes around me, pulling another groan from me. My hands fly to her hips and I squeeze, driving my fingers into her flesh until my knuckles turn white.

"You good?" She has a teasing smirk on her face. She knows exactly what she's doing to me.

I let out a shallow breath. "Yeah. Keep going."

She leans forward, her palms on my chest, her nails digging into my pecs until there's little half-moon indentations in my skin. The new angle has me seeing stars. Her hips lift and then sink back down as mine lift to meet hers. She fucks herself on my cock, riding me like she was meant to do this and nothing else.

I crane my neck up and meet her for a desperate kiss.

She's everywhere, surrounding me. Our bodies are connected in the most intimate of ways, but she's inside of me just as much as I am her. She's clawed her way beneath the surface, shredding my defenses until I've been laid bare before her. And where that should terrify me... I know she'll take good care of me. She won't let anyone or anything hurt me, or come between us, or keep us apart. She'll fight to the last to make sure I'm safe and protected.

I'd do the same for her, no hesitation. She's quickly become an important person in my life. Possibly the most important. I'd move heaven and hell to get to her, to ensure her safety. Her happiness is my highest priority. I love her. I'll do anything for her.

My entire body tenses. I love her. I want to tell her. I *need* to tell her.

But when she swivels her hips and takes me deep inside of her, I know this isn't the right time. Not when there's so many other things to focus on.

The sound of skin slapping skin is loud in the quiet room, punctuated by our pants and sighs and moans. The bed thumps against the wall. I can't make myself care. Not when I have the most perfect woman in my arms, in my bed. Everything else can wait and be dealt with later.

Surging forward, I wrap my arms around her and sit up, forcing her to change her angle. She moves her hands to my shoulders, holding on for balance as she continues to ride me.

The new positioning lets me dip my head and suck her nipple into my mouth. My teeth scrape over the tight bud and she lets out a loud moan.

I let her nipple out of my mouth with a loud pop. "Shh," I tease.

Her face is red and sweaty. She doesn't slow her movements bouncing on my cock like it's her own personal joystick, but she does flip me her middle finger before pushing my face back into her chest.

My hands cup her breasts, bringing them together as I bury my face between them. The day-old stubble lining my cheeks tickles her sensitive skin. When I nibble and suck on the underside of her breasts, Viv lets out a gasp and clenches around my cock so hard I nearly lose it right then and there.

"Oh, fuck," she says, her voice strangled. Her rhythm falters. Her head drops back. "*Fuck.*"

I let her use me, chasing her own pleasure. My thumbs drag over her nipples, playing with the peaks.

"Pinch them. Tug them," she gasps. I do as she directs, kissing up the column of her neck. A bead of sweat drips down the hollow of her throat and I catch it with my tongue, sucking a mark into her skin.

She calls out my name as she comes, her tight channel tightening around me almost to the point of pain. Her hips jerk and twitch as she comes down, her body becoming soft and pliant. She melts into me until I'm the only thing holding her up.

It takes her a few moments to come back to herself, her eyelids heavy. She blinks a few times until she can focus on me. Her happy smile fades as our eyes meet.

I should tell her. I want to tell her.

I love her.

Viv clenches around me. "You didn't come," she whispers.

"Not yet." I thread my hand through her hair, tipping her head back until I can kiss her.

She immediately deepens the kiss, her tongue tangling with mine in a fight for dominance.

I let her win. I'll always let her win.

Sliding my hand down her spine, I flip her onto her back and drive deep inside of her. Her legs wrap around my waist, holding me close.

My hand closes around her ankle, drawing it over my shoulder until her leg is hooked behind my neck. She's folded nearly in half, her breasts pressed tight to my chest as I thrust into her in a steady, punishing pace. The bed frame bangs into the wall over and over, punctuating each thrust with a loud thud.

Sweat slides down my back. The room is heavy with the scent of sex and her perfume, a light, fruity scent that I can't get enough of.

I slide my hand down her flank and around to her spine, then down to her ass. I grab a solid handful and she nips at my lips, never giving up. She might win this battle, but I'll win the war for her heart.

My fingers dig into her ass cheek, creeping inward. I've barely touched her back entrance when she explodes around me, squeezing my cock until I detonate. My release barrels into me, nearly bowling me over. My vision goes black and I think I stop breathing.

As I come down from my high, I become aware of her arms holding me close. I pull out of her and bury my face in her neck, breathing hard. Her heart is pounding against mine, an answering echo.

Vivienne's hand runs through my sweaty hair, pushing back the messy strands. I lift myself up enough to kiss her and she smiles against my lips.

"I think we were a little loud." She looks inordinately pleased with herself.

Pulling myself off her, I make my way to the bathroom to deal with the condom and clean up. When I return to the bed with a wet washcloth, she's drawing the now sweaty, soiled comforter off the bed.

I pull her into my arms, breathing her in. I still can't believe that I get to hold her like this, that she's let me into her life.

Helping her clean up, I drag the wet cloth over her skin, taking care with the bruises on her hips and the reddened beard burn on her chest.

When we climb into the bed, she immediately burrows into me, her arms around my waist and her head on my chest.

"I think I like this," she says.

"Oh?"

"Staying at your house." She looks up at me. "I don't know if your siblings will like it very much."

"They can deal with it." I kiss the tip of her nose. "I like having you here." In my bed, yes, but also in my kitchen and also in my world. She's burrowed her way into my heart.

"I like being here." She lets out a yawn. "Tomorrow is going to suck."

"Sorry." I'm not sorry for keeping her up late. Not when it's so enjoyable for the both of us.

She yawns again. "You'll have to make it up to me."

I kiss the top of her head. "Anytime."

twenty-seven

. . .

Viv

KIANA TAKES one look at me in the locker room and bursts out laughing.

"What?" I ask, turning to look behind me. There's nobody else there.

"Damn, girl," my so-called best friend says. "You got *laid*."

My face heats. "Shut up."

"You're covered in love bites," Grace chimes in. "I'd ask if he tried to eat your entire face, but I'm seeing the proof right now."

"Oh, he ate plenty," I blurt, then cover my face. "I didn't say that."

Cari is across the locker room, getting ready for the day. She shakes her head and smiles.

"You didn't have to hear it," she chimes in. "I thought my earplugs and white noise machine would be enough. They weren't."

"I'm *sorry*," I tell her for the third time.

When I came downstairs for breakfast this morning, Al gave me a sarcastic round of applause and Cari wouldn't meet my eyes. Tony looked proud of himself, the fucker.

"Our Viv is a little loud, huh?" Kiana grins. "Never would have guessed."

"I'm scarred for life," Cari says as she rolls her eyes and smiles.

"Okay, but have you seen him?" I ask the girls. "He's hot as fuck."

"I'm glad he's treating you well," Grace says, slapping my back. "If anyone deserves a little bit of happiness, it's you, Cap. You know you're allowed to relax and have fun sometimes, right?"

"Relax? What's that?" I joke.

Between rugby, working on endorsements, and taking care of my physical health, I don't have much time for *fun*. My monthly get together with my book club is sometimes the only time I get to take a load off. I don't know the last time I took the time for a bubble bath.

Kiana frowns. "You need to take time for yourself too. You can't always put the rest of us ahead."

"I'll try." My promise is empty and we all know it.

Although with Tony going away for a few weeks… Now is as good a time as any to practice some self-care.

He leaves tomorrow for the Netherlands and the competition. The time difference isn't terrible—it's not like he's going to Australia, where they hosted the competition last year—but it's the first time we'll be apart for more than twenty-four hours since we started dating.

It hasn't been very long, but I've grown accustomed to sleeping beside him every night. I don't know what I'm going to do without him. It's crazy how quickly I've become addicted to him.

And it's more than the sex. Yeah, that's great. He's always attentive, always makes sure my pleasure is a priority. I never feel uncomfortable or unappreciated.

The way he supports me—emotionally, yes, but also with my goals, with pushing myself to be better, to do better. He works himself to the bone, but he's never made me feel like I'm not important. He's made clear that he values me and wants me in his life. I wish I could show him how important he is to me.

The team gathers on the pitch for training. For once, I'm on top of things. I play some of the best rugby of my life in our scrimmage. And after, when we hit the weights room, I feel like I can achieve anything.

"So you're coming with us, right?" Kiana says, slinging her arm around my shoulders as we head back to the locker room.

"Going where?"

"The cute new diner down the road," Grace chimes in.

"Sure, I can do that."

Tony's at the shelter for another few hours, helping the vet tech with a bunch of immunizations. It's not like I have anything else on my agenda for the day.

After a refreshing shower, I put on clean clothes and throw my wet hair into a quick braid before gathering with the rest of the girls. There are seven of us going for a late lunch.

I meant it when I told Cari these girls are my sisters. They're my family. Things have been a bit different lately, but just because I have a boyfriend now doesn't mean I'm not wholly devoted to them. To us.

While I'm thinking about it, I pull out my phone and send a quick "hi, I'm alive" to my siblings' group chat. Chuck and Perry use it mostly to taunt each other, Bradley almost never responds, Janine never has her phone on her, and Frankie will send memes and gifs in response to every single question she's asked.

It feels like the responsibility falls on my shoulders to moderate it, to make sure everyone's okay. My therapist says that's an oldest child trait and not particularly healthy. It's not my job to ensure everyone else is eating right and training hard and feeling comfortable in their skin. It's not *bad* to care about them; but it's not my responsibility to manage their lives for them. I have to let them live and either thrive or fail on their own. It's hard. I want to protect my little siblings, even though they're all adults who can take care of themselves.

Knowing Tony is the same way… I feel a little guilty for stealing him away from his siblings the last two weeks. They don't get much time together and I've been hoarding him for myself.

I enjoyed our dinner and a movie last night. As long as they're okay with having me there, I'll make sure we split our time a little more evenly between our places. I don't want them to resent me for taking him away from them.

Lunch goes a long way toward refilling my energy tank. I didn't realize how much I needed this social time with my girls. Thankfully, there's more interesting conversation than my sex life.

Kiana is worried about her aging grandfather, who recently had a bad fall. Grace and her wife had a fight. And to my surprise, Cari tells us she's having difficulty adjusting to the new team dynamic.

"It's not that I don't love you guys," she adds quickly. "I just… I was at school for four years. I knew those girls like I knew myself. And now I don't have that support network or the structure to my day. I'm just… I'm struggling."

Reaching across the table, I take her hand in mine. "We'll help you get through this."

"What can we do to help?" Kiana adds.

Practice times fluctuate throughout the week. It's not set it stone; each week is different, and it will only get worse when we start adding games to our schedule. It's not like we can change the externalized structure for her. She has to come up with a system that works for her.

Cari swallows. "I don't know."

"That's okay," I tell her. "You don't have to figure it out all at once. It's okay to trial and error."

She buries her face in her hands. To my horror, she bursts into tears.

"I'm just so overwhelmed. I don't know if I can do this."

I'm out of my seat in an instant. Rounding the table, I pull her into my arms, and she buries her face in my neck. She clings to me, shaking like a leaf as she cries.

"I can't do this."

And at that moment, Tony walks into the diner. He stops short at the sight of his sister crying.

"What's wrong?" His voice is thunderous, his features hard and sharp.

Cari sobs.

"It's okay," I rub her back soothingly, trying to block out the way he's glaring daggers at me. "You don't have to figure it all out at once."

"I should know by now."

"No. Don't think like that." My hands on her shoulders, I draw her back until our eyes meet. "There's no timeline that says you have to know everything exactly as it's supposed to be for the rest of your life. You're allowed to change and grow, and you're allowed space to consider everything. Just because it's hard right now doesn't mean it always will be. And just because something is easy for one person doesn't mean it's not difficult for everyone else."

A tear trails down her cheek.

"It's okay to not be okay," I tell her quietly. "It's okay to seek help. And it's okay to work through things on your own."

"I just want..." Cari sighs. "I don't know what I want. I want to *know* what I want."

Letting out a small laugh, I tug her into a hug. "I feel that. I think we've all been there at one point or another."

"I just don't like feeling this way." She rubs at her eyes

with the back of her hand. "It feels… itchy. Like there's something wrong with me."

"There's nothing wrong with you," I tell her seriously. "And whatever you're struggling with—you have a whole team to support you. There's a whole squad ready to do battle for you. Even if that battle is within yourself."

Cari swallows, rubbing at her eyes again. "Sorry for being a big ol' crybaby."

"Girl, please." Grace gets up and joins us, wrapping her arm around Cari's shoulders. "I started crying last week because I finished my can of protein powder. If anything, *I'm* the crybaby."

"I cried when I got my period," Andi adds. "I freaking hate wearing tampons. I've been getting my period for twenty years and I still cry every fucking month."

Cari gives a teary laugh. "I cry when I get my period too. Though usually it's out of relief."

Andi grins at her. "See? We're twins."

Gently, I steer her back to her chair. "You'll be okay," I tell her. "We've got your back. On the field and off."

I chance a glance at Tony's face. He still has that hard set to his jaw, but his eyes are softening.

Behind him are Brody and another guy. Probably one of his teammates. I think I recognize him from the gym last week. I don't know; I only had eyes for one gymnast.

"What're you guys doing here?" Cari asks her brother.

"Vivienne invited me." He steps forward and kisses the top of her head. "You're okay?" His voice is gruff.

"I will be," she says with a sniff.

"Hold on," Kiana interrupts. "You call her *Vivienne*?"

"It's her name," he says, glaring at her.

Brody pulls up two chairs, the third guy grabbing another.

Tony settles beside me, his arm sliding around my shoulders. His fingers on my chin, he tilts my head to kiss me.

All the tension coiled tight inside of me evaporates. There

are times I have to be strong and capable, but when I'm with him, I don't feel the weight of that responsibility on my shoulders. I feel like I can breathe, like I only have to worry about taking care of myself and not everyone around me.

"Viv," Brody says. "Nice to see you again."

"You too."

"I'm Dylan," the other guy says, offering his hand for a shake. "I don't think we've had a chance to chat. I really like what you've done the last few weeks."

"Oh?"

"The big grump has a heart," he teases. "It's nice to see him smile."

Tony glowers at him, so I smile enough for the both of us.

"I like it too."

The girls go around and introduce themselves. A few of them met Brody when he and Tony dropped by practice, but the guys didn't linger.

And now that I know it was all a ploy for Tony to ask me out… yeah, I'm not upset about that in the slightest.

It's nice for our friends and teammates to mingle. I hope they all get along. It's as important to me as Tony's siblings and my siblings getting along. These girls are my sisters too.

My boyfriend tightens his arm around me and steals a sweet potato fry off my plate. He goes to pop it into his mouth when, at the last moment, he detours and offers it to me instead. My smile stretches wide across my face as I let him feed me.

"You're disgusting," Grace says with a grin.

"Disgustingly happy, maybe," Kiana chimes in.

"You're right about that," I tell them.

With a laugh, I lean into Tony and he kisses my temple. I don't know a time I've ever been so happy.

twenty-eight

. . .

Tony

ROTTERDAM. I've never been to the Netherlands before. It's such a funny name, I half believed it doesn't even exist except, one, I got an A in my college geography class, and two, the women's gymnastics team is one of the best in the world. They've won the bronze medal at the last two Worlds competitions.

We're six hours ahead of Boston. I sent Viv and my siblings a text—separately—when we landed, but now that we're in the hotel and supposed to be getting settled, all I'm doing is getting more *unsettled*.

We have three days of training and to get used to the time difference before the opening ceremonies. Then it will be a whirlwind four days of qualification rounds before the six days of finals competition.

Two and a half weeks is a *long* time to be away from home. Luckily, Susan at the shelter and my boss at the restaurant were understanding. They know this is what I've been working toward for the last several months. Years, really. I've put so many hours of dedication into my sport. I'm one of the best gymnasts in the world; that's why I'm at the *World* Championships.

Now I have to prove it: to everyone else, but also to myself.

Brody and I are sharing a room for the duration of the competition. He immediately collapses onto one of the beds and passes out, but I can't sleep. I'm wide awake.

Yesterday, Viv and I recorded three videos for Pump It Up Protein. We stood side by side as we talked through the script, making our own shakes. Then we clinked the cups together for a *cheers* and that was it. There was nothing intimate, nothing about our relationship—except the fact that we were there on camera together.

She posted the first video after I got on the plane and it automatically shared to my page. My phone keeps buzzing with notifications. Already, over two thousand people have commented on the video.

It baffles me how many people are tuning in to watch her. Not that she isn't great; she's absolutely fantastic. It's more how invested they are in *us*. They didn't care about me before. I don't know that they really care about me now, except for a desire to know more about her.

If I have this platform, I'm going to do my best to show the world what gymnastics is all about. Women's gymnastics gets a lot of splashy attention at the Olympics, but men's gymnastics doesn't draw the same viewers. We share enough commonality that the people who tune in every four years should be able to understand at least a little bit of what's going on.

And hey, even if they only watch the women's gymnastics at Worlds, it's still more viewers. More people who pay attention to gymnastics as a whole. The important part is growing the sport. Getting more people watching and participating. If I can give back even a fraction of what gymnastics has given me, I'll be happy.

I make my way through the hotel to the small garden outside. We're in the middle of the city center, surrounded by old buildings interspersed with new construction. There's a chill to the air. November in northwestern Europe is just as cold as Boston. My Team USA warmup hoodie is no match for the weather.

My phone vibrates with a text. It's Viv.

> I'm sure you're exhausted. I just wanted to tell you that you're going to kick ass. However you do in this competition, no matter how many medals you do or don't bring home, my feelings for you won't change. Your worth is not based on your performance.

My heart jumps into my throat. My fingers type out half a dozen messages before I delete them. I love you. I love you. I love you.

But telling her over text is not the way to do this.

I almost said it during sex the other night. I almost blurted it out at lunch with her teammates. And when we went back to her place and we were laying sweaty and sated in her bed, I almost said it again.

She deserves better. She deserves to hear the words for the first time face to face. I never want her to feel like an afterthought, like she isn't the single most important person in my life.

Because she is. There's no doubt in my mind that Viv is it for me. She's my future. I want to grow old with her. Whatever that looks like— marriage or no rings, kids or no kids, I want her by my side. Whatever her next step is, I want to be by her side.

When I retire from gymnastics, whether I make it to the Olympics next summer or not... I'll have done so knowing I gave it my all. I'm ready to move on to new things. Vet school. A new career. The next chapter in my life.

And if I play my cards right, hopefully she'll be there right alongside me.

———

If I thought the weeks leading up to Worlds was a lot, it's nothing compared to the amount of training and focus that actually being at the competition involves. Even though I've been doing this for most of life, even though I've been to two prior Worlds competitions plus the Olympics, I'm still overwhelmed by how exhausting everything is.

After spending all day in the gym, I collapse into my bed and pass out. Brody's snores on the other side of the room don't even register.

The opening ceremony passes in the blink of an eye. I barely hear the cheering crowds as each team is introduced to great fanfare. With every fiber of my being, I wish Vivienne could be here. I understand why she isn't; she's training, it's a job for her just like it is for me. Cari is working right alongside her. Al has games he can't miss to jaunt halfway across the world. My parents can't leave my aging *abuela* to come cheer me on.

Brody's girlfriend and Dylan's boyfriend came along for the trip. They have tickets in the stands, since they aren't allowed to be on the competition floor. Only the team staff can be on the floor with us.

The first round of qualifiers is for the team, then we'll have individual event competition for each apparatus. Dylan has a fantastic day on the rings and Brody nails his high bar routine. When it comes time for me to do my vault, I step up to the podium and let out a shaky exhale.

All of my training, all the blood and sweat and tears; it all comes down to this.

My eyes close for a moment as I try to calibrate. I can practically hear Viv, her steady voice telling me I can do this. I catch a whiff of strawberries and almost believe she's there.

Coach Jack claps me on the shoulder. "You've got this," he says before he steps back.

Saluting the judges, I take my place at the end of the runway. My heart pounds.

One more breath.

And then I jump into my run, racing down toward the table. I hit the springboard for my round-off and back handspring, then launch off the vault and twist in the air.

One, two, three times I twist, adding an extra half twist at the end.

My feet crash into the padded mat and I use every muscle within me to keep my balance. It takes everything I have, but with only the smallest step, I manage to stay on my feet.

I did it. I landed the vault.

Blood rushes through my veins and I hear the cheers of the crowd. The noise hits me like a punch to the face. Before, I was able to block it out and focus. Now, it's all I can hear.

"Great job, man," Brody says, giving me a fist bump as I rejoin the team.

"Good one," Tommy adds in with a bump of his own.

"Thanks."

I cut the tape off my wrists as we watch Dylan do his vault.

When my score comes up, Coach Ross claps me on the back. "Good job," he says, pride in his voice.

Gymnastics scores consist of two numbers: difficulty and execution. Execution counts down from a ten, whereas difficulty is open-ended. In the current code of points, it's one of the most difficult, but because of that, it's awarded one of the highest starting values.

My score is currently second in the competition. Out of twenty-four teams and five gymnasts apiece, I'm second.

Fuck. I'll take that.

Shaking out my wrists, I try to breathe and bleed off the adrenaline coursing through my system.

And that's when I spot her in the crowd.

Vivienne.

She's holding a poster board sign that says *stick the landing and I'll nail you* and has a smile stretching from ear to ear. She's *here*.

All of my aches and pains fade away. All the noise dims.

She's here. She flew halfway around the world to be here. For me.

My sister is standing beside her, but I barely register her presence.

"You can't be here," the security guard barks, holding them back. "The floor is for athletes only."

Grabbing a folding chair from our team's section, I drag it over to the barricade, then hop up. We're almost level now.

"Hi," I whisper.

"Hi." She bites her lip. "I hope it's okay I'm here."

My mouth goes dry. "Very okay."

"I missed you," she says quietly.

My heart gives a painful thump.

"I love you."

Her eyes go wide. "What?"

"I love you," I repeat. "I'm so fucking glad that you're here."

Reaching for her, I pull her as close as I can before I kiss her. I'm perched precariously on the edge of the chair, my weight balanced on the barricade. If I fall and break my leg, so be it. It'll be worth it for this moment.

Viv kisses me back, her arms winding around my neck.

"I love you too," she murmurs against my lips.

I pull back. "Say it again."

"I love you." Vivienne's eyes are bright and her lips are puffy and red from kissing me. "I love you."

twenty-nine

. . .

Viv

"BRODY," I announce when we get back to the hotel. "You need to clear out."

He pouts. "You can't kick me out of my own room."

"You don't get to watch this." Tony glares at him, his arm slung around my waist. "Now leave."

Brody grins as he pretends to grumble. I'm sure he's off to visit his girlfriend and do the exact same thing we're about to do.

Once the door closes behind him, Tony flips the deadbolt, then pulls me back into his arms.

"Say it again." His eyes are trained on mine.

"I love you." I wind my arms around his neck. "I love you."

"Fuck, Vivienne." His voice is hoarse. "I love you so fucking much."

"Show me."

Walking backward, I pull him with me toward the bed. He reaches for the hem of my shirt, yanking it over my shoulders unceremoniously, then slips his fingers beneath the waistband of my leggings. His eyes meet mine for consent and, when I nod, he pulls the spandex over my hips and down my thighs.

I help kick them off until I'm left in my bra and underwear, his piercing gaze burning me from within.

Tony settles between my legs. He kisses my fabric-covered pussy, his tongue telling me exactly what he wants to do with me.

But he doesn't take off my panties. I arch beneath his touch, desperate for more. He doesn't hurry up.

Taking matters into my own hands, I shove the fabric off my hips. He helps pull the scrap of satin down my legs, leaving a kiss on the inside of my knee. *Finally*, he touches me. He flings my underwear over his shoulder before he dives in and licks me.

I let out a stuttered moan. My hands find his hair almost on instinct, running my fingers through the silky strands.

We've done this enough that he knows exactly what I like, what I need. The rough scrape of his stubble on the inside of my thighs makes me shiver. I'm sure I'll be walking funny later. Totally worth it.

Tony slides two fingers inside of me, the unexpected stretch making me arch my back as I adjust. I want more. I need more. He withdraws and then thrusts his fingers inside, the glide made smooth by my natural wetness, as he continues to lick and suck on my clit. The steady pressure and suction of his mouth combined with the rhythm of his fingers make everything inside of me coil tight like a spring.

My fingers dig into his shoulders as I ride his face. He makes an appreciative hum, the vibration reverberating through me. It doesn't take long for me to reach the peak, and as he shows me exactly how much he loves me, I vow to do the same for him. Always.

I barely have time to gasp before the orgasm hits me. As pleasure courses through my veins, a pleasant warmth floods my system, warring with the natural oxytocin.

He loves me. I'm not too much for him. He loves me exactly as I am.

And that feels fucking *magical*.

Tony pulls his fingers out of me and brings them to his lips, sucking them clean. I fucking *whimper* as my blood heats. His eyes darken as he smirks at me like he knows exactly what he's doing.

Grabbing him by the shoulders, I pull him up the bed until he's on top of me. He pulls me into his arms, his hard cock nudging the inside of my thigh. He makes no effort to move things along. He's learned I need some cuddling time before I'm ready to continue.

My hand cups his cheek as I kiss him. The taste of me on his lips makes me clench around the emptiness deep within me. My hips rock against his involuntarily, the slight friction of his body hair a tease against my sensitive skin.

"Shit." Tony goes tense.

"What's wrong?"

"I don't have any condoms."

Right. He was going on a three-week work trip. It's probably a good thing he didn't pack any. There would never be a situation where he would need them.

My face falls. "I didn't think to bring any."

I know I should have been more prepared, but when I booked the first flight out of town, I threw a few things into a backpack and hopped on the plane. I didn't *plan*.

My stomach twists. "We could…"

"It's okay," he says, pulling me close. "There are plenty of other ways I can get you off."

"Or… We could skip them." My stomach swoops. "We've both got our test results back. I'm on birth control. It's not…"

His eyes darken. "You'd go without? With me?"

"I want to feel you. All of you."

I've never risked going without a condom before. My periods have always been irregular. I've been on birth control forever, starting the medication years before I became sexually active to help regulate things. Condoms protect against more than just unexpected pregnancy. Even seeing a partner's test results didn't make me feel comfortable.

Until now, I've never felt truly safe in a relationship. There's always been a power imbalance. My star has always shined brighter and that meant my ex-partners would try to overcompensate. It didn't leave me feeling good about myself. There's a reason none of those relationships worked out.

He doesn't care about that. He doesn't care that I'm in the spotlight and doesn't try to steal that spotlight for himself. He doesn't want to use me to prop himself up. And he doesn't have an interest in one-upping me in any way.

He respects me, period. I've never had that before. I didn't really believe it was possible—until now.

Tony threads his fingers through my hair, kissing me roughly. The heat in his kiss makes me light up inside. Warmth builds in my chest as I wrap my arms more tightly around him. His muscles flex and bulge beneath his tattoos, making the designs ripple.

I could spend hours cataloguing the fine lines and colors of the ink. One day, I'll ask him to tell me the story behind each one, when he got them, the meaning behind them. One day, I'll know everything there is to know about him.

And where before, that might have scared me... Now, I'm ready for it. I want to know everything.

My hands slide down his back to his ass, my fingers digging into the firm flesh. One day, we'll have to see whose ass is better. My thighs are probably stronger than his, but his arm muscles put mine to shame. He can't tackle though, and there's no way I could do one twist or flip, much less as many as he does. There's a reason we're better at different things. If we were exactly the same, it wouldn't be half as much fun.

When Tony kisses that spot beneath the hinge of my jaw, I melt into a puddle in his arms. He smiles against my skin and his cock nudges the inside of my thigh again.

"You're sure about this?" His voice is gravelly, as rough as sandpaper.

Nodding, I make sure to meet his eyes. "I've never been more sure of anything."

He pulls back slightly, working a hand between us until the head of his cock is at my entrance. I prop myself up on my elbow so I can watch as he slides bare inside of me.

The thick, blunt head is shiny with pre-cum, and as I stretch around him with nothing between us, the heat of him lights me up from inside.

Tony's eyes flutter shut and he has to work to keep them open. I cup his cheek, the rough scrape of his stubble on my palm grounding me.

He snaps his hips forward, filling me in one fluid thrust, and now it's my eyes rolling back in my head. Letting out a soft grunt, he drops down again until our torsos are touching, my breasts pressed to his chest.

"I love you," he murmurs into my ear.

Automatically, I clench around him, and he groans.

"I love that too," he says, laughter in his voice. He gives an experimental thrust of his hips, the smooth glide of his cock sending pleasure through me. "But I love you more."

"I love you more," I counter, my hips rocking against his. I've said the words before, but I've never meant them so wholeheartedly. Before, it might have been puppy love. Now I know what true love feels like. I know what I stand to lose. I don't ever want to live without him.

He fucks me slowly, like he needs to commit this to memory as much as I do. His kiss tells me all the ways he's going to love me.

Grabbing hold of his hand, I lace our fingers together. Somehow, it feels even more intimate than his bare cock moving inside of me. He squeezes my hand like he's afraid to let go.

"Vivienne," he whispers, before he buries his face in my neck.

I cup the back of his head, my hands sifting through the fine strands. His rhythm falters.

"Please," he says. "I can't hold back. I need you to come."

It's not like I can control it. I'd like to come too.

"Roll over," I tell him.

He slides out of me, moving onto his back. I straddle him and then sink onto his cock, the familiar fullness sending electricity down my spine.

Tony's hands settle on my hips, his thumb skating over my clit. Mine land on his abs as I fuck myself on his cock, taking what I need from him. He does his best to keep up with me, thrusting up into me.

He leans forward, catching my breast in his grasp and sucking my nipple into his mouth. All it takes is a scrape of his teeth against the sensitive bud before the orgasm hits me. I clench around him, my pussy throbbing around his cock, and when I throw my head back to ride the waves of pleasure, he groans and jerks beneath me.

The flood of his release inside of me is a new sensation. I collapse onto his chest, his arms coming up to hold me close. As his cock starts to soften and slip out of me, I can feel his cum leaking, too. I... I think I like it. His mark is branded deep within me now. He's claimed me in a way nobody else ever has—or ever will.

Breathing heavily, Tony kisses my temple, his arms tight around me.

"I love you," he murmurs, like he's afraid I've forgotten.

I haven't. I never will. How could I possibly forget the best thing to ever happen to me?

"I love you too."

thirty

. . .

Tony

WHEN THEY PUT the team silver medal around my neck, I have to clench my jaw before I start crying like a baby. I'm not ashamed of crying. But once I start crying, I won't stop, and nobody needs to take photographs for the international press with my face all blotchy and my eyes swollen. I'll save that for the team party in a few hours.

With the fancy podium lights, I can't see her, but I know Viv is in the crowd cheering me on.

I've placed into the event finals for my two best events. After a day off for rest, I'll have the vault final competition, and then two days later will be the floor finals. However I do, wherever I place, I'll have done my best.

All of this has reignited my fire for gymnastics. I thought I was done. I'm ready to move on to the next phase of my life. But I don't think gymnastics is quite done with *me*.

I'm going to make a solid run at the Olympic team. If I don't make it, I'll walk away with my head held high. But if I make it… I'll finish my fifteen years of elite competitive gymnastics at the pinnacle of my sport.

I've had a storybook career. Two—now *three*—World Championships team medals. Two World silver medals on vault and a bronze on floor. An Olympic bronze team medal. Not to mention the fistfuls of medals I've won over the years.

Athletes fight through adversity. It's what we do. We do what we have to do. I like to think I've proven it to be true. Through working my ass off at my three jobs, taking care of my siblings, and generally figuring out who I am and what I stand for, I've been able to consistently perform with the best in the world. I've made it to the upper echelon.

After the official medal ceremony is over, the team gathers in our conference room at the hotel. The women's gymnastics team is here as well—their team competition is tomorrow, and they're poised to win gold for the umpteenth time in a row, but the Russians and Canadians are pulling close in qualification scores and Brazil and Romania aren't far behind. It'll be a good meet to watch, that's for sure.

I make a beeline for Viv, who immediately wraps me in a hug.

"I love you," I whisper in her ear. "Thank you for being here."

"I wouldn't miss it for the world," she says.

She won't always be able to be at all of my meets, just like I won't be able to make it to all of her matches. Our schedules won't always line up perfectly. I've already looked ahead at the calendar—her first match of the season is the same weekend as the Winter Cup, the men's start of season competition.

But wherever we can, however we can, we'll be there for each other. We'll support each other.

Anxiety gnaws at my stomach when I think beyond next summer. It's time to start applying to vet schools. I really don't want to leave Boston, but if I have to... Will she come with me? That's a lot of pressure to put on a new relationship. Especially considering how much her life will be changing without rugby in it...

I can't borrow trouble. We'll deal with that later, when it

becomes more time sensitive. I don't want to make it a problem before it needs to be.

Going through the retirement process with someone else, making all these big lifestyle adjustments with someone going through the exact same thing at the same time... I think it'll make us stronger. From what my former teammates have all said, it's not an easy process. Doing it together, I think we'll be able to handle it. We can handle anything as long as we're doing it together.

With Viv tucked under my arm, I introduce her to the athletes and the support staff she hasn't met. Coach Jack greets her with a wide smile. Ross is less friendly—I'm guessing he remembers her dropping by the training facility.

There are a few guests of Team USA, people related to the team or associated with the sport.

I'm surprised when Viv greets Charlotte Kent with a happy smile. I've known Charlotte for years just from being involved in the highest echelon of the sport, but I didn't realize they were friends. Then again, she *was* at the restaurant with that group last week.

"Congratulations," Charlotte says with a pleased smile. She gives me a quick hug. "I thought something was up with you two the other night, but seeing you in person... I'm so happy for you."

"Thanks. I'm happy for us too." I press a kiss to Viv's temple. "She's pretty fantastic."

Vivienne scoffs, lightly backhanding my chest, and I grab her hand and squeeze.

"You are."

Her face flushes. "You're ridiculous."

"I really think this new partnership is going to be good," Charlotte continues. "Birdie is doing everything right."

Oh. That's their sponsor. Birdie Sportswear was hosting the dinner the other night.

"We'll have to arrange a get together the week of the

shoot," Viv says. "I'd love to work with your She Can Fly campaign."

Charlotte goes around the country talking about getting girls involved in sports. She's a UNICEF ambassador, a *Sports Illustrated* cover model, and generally an all-around lovely person. She's also fairly open about her history with an eating disorder. If there's anyone Viv can lean on to navigate the post-rugby world, Charlotte would be an excellent ally.

"That would be great." Charlotte gives her a genuine smile and my grumpy girlfriend beams.

We mingle throughout the room. Cari is deep in conversation with Brody's girlfriend and Dylan's boyfriend. My teammates are talking with some of the other athletes from the women's, rhythmic, and mixed trampoline teams.

A wave of happiness settles over me. Being around all the people important to me… the only thing that would make it better would be if Al and my parents could be here, but I understand why they couldn't make it. They've already texted their support and congratulations.

The job isn't done. I've helped the team earn a medal, but now it's time for me to do it on my own.

thirty-one

. . .

Viv

IT ABSOLUTELY KILLS me that I'm on a plane when Tony wins his gold medal. I've paid through the nose for in-flight Wi-Fi and Charlotte is live-texting me the scores, but I can't actually be there in person. I don't know if I can ever forgive myself.

Tony insisted it didn't matter to him. I was lucky to get three days away from the team over our weekend off. There's still a risk I'll face discipline for skipping practice the other day. That's a chance I'll have to take. Being there for his competitions whenever I can, however I can, I'll support him.

Even if it's on a plane ride.

When I land in Boston, my phone lights up. Alycia's sent me photos of his medal ceremony. He joked he was an ugly crier and the pictures don't lie; his face is red and splotchy, his eyes swollen as they place the gold medal around his neck.

I start to tear up. The pure emotion on his face overwhelms me. This is what he's worked for all these years, and seeing it come to fruition is recognition of all the work he's put in for the last twenty years. Even though I couldn't be there in the moment, I feel like I've been there with him for this too.

The girls rib me at practice over skipping town, the coaches shake their heads, and life goes on.

Every morning, I wake up alone in my bed. I make a protein shake using Pump It Up Protein and text Tony a photo, wishing he could be there with me but knowing why he can't. I wouldn't want him to give up a single moment of this competition, especially knowing it will be his last. He wouldn't want me to sacrifice my career for him, and I feel the exact same way.

It sucks to be apart. But this is the job, and there's a finite end to it. It won't be like this forever.

So despite counting down the days and then the hours until we can be together again, I live my life. A night out at book club, brunch with my teammates…

And when my brother comes into town for his game against the Grizzlies, I visit him too. He left my name with the arena staff, but before I can pull out my ID to check in, I hear my name called.

"Viv!"

Al is wearing a Grizzlies T-shirt and athletic shorts. He crosses the players' entrance lobby and tugs me into a hug.

"How was Rotterdam?" he asks, tugging me past the guard with a nod.

"It was good. He did so well."

"I'm so proud of him," he says quietly. "I wish I could have been there."

I squeeze his arm. "He knows why you weren't."

He was on a road trip to Detroit and then Toronto. They just got home yesterday.

"So, what brings you to my little corner?" Al gives me a cheeky grin. "You ready to dump that oaf?"

I laugh. "Your brother isn't an oaf."

His eyes sparkle with laughter. "Oh, so you're here to see *your* oaf of a brother?"

"Something like that."

Al gasps playfully. "You traitor."

"Nope. I'm neutral."

"Please tell me you will at least wear my sweater tonight," Al begs as we approach the visitor's training area.

"I think your brother might have an issue with me wearing a different Gonzales on my back."

"We have the same name." He waves it away. "Now, if you wore Larsson's sweater, he might have a problem with it, but I'm family."

"Yeah, but Chuck's my baby brother."

Al laughs loudly. "You hear that, Gallagher?" There are a few guys in Colorado Dragons T-shirts kicking a soccer ball around, my brother with them. "You're her baby brother."

"Fuck off," Chuck says with a scowl on his face.

Al grins. "You really are related!"

Laughing, I give Al a quick hug. "Thanks for making sure I got here safely."

"I'll see you after the game," he promises. "I'll be the good-looking Gonzales brother."

Chuck snorts. "You really think that?"

My brother opens his arms and I hug him. He's taller than me, wider than me, and overall stronger than me, but he's still a softy at heart.

"You look good, Viv," he says quietly.

"I feel really good." I pull back to look him over.

There's a definite family resemblance. We share the same dark hair and sharp facial features. He has green eyes—and his twin's are blue—whereas I have brown. He keeps his hair short and his beard neatly maintained.

"How have you been?" I catalog the exhaustion on his face, the weariness in his eyes.

"I'm okay," he says, his voice lacking some of its usual warmth.

"Just okay?" I pinch his chin in my fingers, studying him more closely.

"My girl and I broke up," Chuck finally says, his eyes darting away from mine.

"I didn't know you were dating anyone."

"Well, it wasn't serious. We weren't social media official," he says defensively. He sighs. "I'm sorry. I don't mean to snap. I just miss her."

Curling my arms around him, I wrap him in a hug. "I'm sorry, Chucky."

"Yeah, me too." He hugs me close. "I'll be okay. It's still fresh."

"Anything I can do to help?"

He chuckles sadly. "Maybe don't mention it in the group chat?"

"You've got it."

"Come on," he says. "Let me introduce you to the team."

He's been with Colorado for three seasons now, so I've met a few of his teammates before, and they say hello and offer hugs or handshakes. He introduces me to the players I haven't met.

"So you're friends with the Grizzlies," Chuck says slowly as he leads me to the dining room, where a few catering trays are laid out. I fix myself a cup of tea as he grabs a sandwich.

"I guess so. A few of my friends are dating people on the team."

"And Gonzales," he points out.

I roll my eyes. "You mean my boyfriend's brother?"

"Yeah. He seemed awfully friendly."

"That's just Al."

Chuck is quiet for a moment. "I'm glad you have him in your corner."

"I am too."

"It's hard. Being away from everyone." He sighs. "I know I have Janine in town, but I don't get to see her much. Perry's in the middle of his season. Frankie never returns my calls. And Bradley… I don't know what to do with him."

"There's nothing to do," I tell him. "He's living his life. It's not your job to manage him, or any of the rest of them."

He looks away. "I miss Perry."

"Me too."

"No, like…" He sighs. "It's different with us."

"The twin thing?"

"I've always been able to manage the distance. I would never want to come between him and his career," Chuck says. "I just wish his career and mine didn't mean we're fifteen hundred miles apart."

"Have you thought about asking for a trade? Raleigh has an NHL team…"

He shakes his head. "Denver isn't going to trade me. And I'm halfway certain that as soon as I get settled wherever he is, he's going to up and sign somewhere else. Like he did when you were living with him."

"That's not the same thing. He was traded." As sad as I was to see him leave the comfortable life we'd built here, I knew it wasn't something either of us could control.

And I'd never want to hold my brother back. Any of my siblings. I want us all to climb the highest mountains and crush our goals.

"Sometimes people move away, they have new priorities in their lives," I tell my brother. "It doesn't mean they stop loving you. It just means their priorities have shifted."

He grunts, like he doesn't quite believe me. "I guess."

"You will always be twins. You'll always be brothers. Nothing will take that away."

Chuck shakes his head. "Logically, I know that, but…"

"But it still hurts to realize he's not your number one phone call," I finish.

"Yeah. It's silly. We've been living in different cities since we went off to college. And it's not like we were attached at the hip during breaks." My brother sighs. "I miss the stupid butthead."

I roll my eyes. "Have you told him?"

He stares at me. "What?"

"Have you picked up the phone and called him? Or texted? *Hey, my girlfriend and I just broke up and I'm deep in my feels, can you please be there for me?*"

He blinks a few times. "No?" His voice goes up an octave. "Why would I do that?"

It's my turn to shake my head. "You're kind of dumb sometimes, Chucky. He has no idea you're feeling like this. You have to tell him. Open and honest communication is the bedrock of all relationships."

He makes a face. "Ew, gross. You know I'm allergic to feelings."

"Charles Lawrence Gallagher, you are not allergic to feelings," I snap. "Trust me. Six weeks ago, the thought of talking shit out would make me break out in hives. You're nowhere near as bad as I was. Call your brother and tell him you fucking miss him."

"How'd you get through it?" Chuck asks. "How'd you stop with the hives?"

The thought of Tony makes me smile, and he nods knowingly.

"Ah. The sex?"

Balling up a napkin, I toss it at him. "No, you goofball. He loves me. He wants me to succeed. And I love him back. I support him like he's supporting me."

"So when do I get to meet him?"

I check my watch, even though I already know. "His flight lands in a few hours. He'll be at the game tonight."

"Great," Chuck says with a toothy grin. "I can't wait to meet the guy who made my grumpy sister turn into a lovesick fool."

thirty-two

· · ·

Tony

THERE'S a naked Vivienne in my bed.

Dropping my bag on the floor, I make my way over to the sleeping beauty. I kiss her forehead and she stirs.

"Hey," she says sleepily, her eyes fluttering open and then falling shut again. She reaches clumsily for me, her arms grasping at nothing. "I was waiting for you."

"I missed you." I kiss her softly. "You nap. I'll be here when you wake up."

"I'm awake," she says, but her eyes don't open.

Chuckling under my breath, I pull the covers up around her and make my way into the en-suite. A quick shower later, I've gotten all the plane germs off me, and I crawl naked into the bed beside her. She immediately rolls over and snuggles into me.

Before I pass out, I set an alarm for two hours. There's only enough time for a quick nap.

I drift off into a hazy dream. There's something about dinosaurs riding clouds of sparkles, the color green, and the sound of the ocean. A pulse of lust runs through me, which is weird. I'm in that weird liminal space where I can recognize something is off, but not quite able to understand why.

Warm, wet suction engulfs my cock. My eyelids feel like they're covered in cement. Something soft and wet teases my balls. I thrust involuntarily and a muffled gasp makes me finally open my eyes.

Vivienne is naked, her hand wrapped around my cock, my balls in her mouth as she strokes me. She looks up at me and smirks before she takes my cock into her mouth, her tongue swirling over the sensitive head.

With uncoordinated limbs, I reach down and cup her cheek, trying wordlessly to tell her all the thoughts in my head.

"Love you," I murmur, and she smiles around my cock.

We'd agreed to this beforehand; she's allowed to wake me up by touching me or sucking me, but any actual penetration would have to wait until we were both awake and able to consent. Likewise, if I were to wake her up with my head between her legs, she's good with it as long as I don't use my fingers inside of her.

Limits are important. Boundaries are crucial. It might be awkward to talk about sometimes, but it will make us stronger.

"C'mere." I try to pull her up. She tightens her grip on my cock, her mouth paying attention to that sensitive vein beneath the head. I let out a groan and my head drops back. "Fuck, Vivienne. Your mouth…"

She plays with my balls, then slides two fingers back to rub against my taint. Pleasure erupts down my spine. I bolt upright in a hurry.

"If you don't stop, I'm going to come," I tell her seriously. "I don't want to come in your mouth."

Viv pulls off. She straddles me instead, positioning the head of my cock at her entrance.

I frown. "I didn't—you aren't—"

Her hot, wet cunt spasms as she slides down my length. "I'm good," she says.

"You get to come first. Every time."

She shakes her head. "It's not a checklist. This feels good. I'm good," she says firmly.

She lifts up and slides back down, my hips rising to meet hers. She lets out a shuddery breath.

"Besides, we don't have time. You can get me off again later."

"Deal." I pull her down on top of me. My hips punch up, thrusting into her. "As long as after is all the time."

"I want to feel you inside of me," she says. "I want it to leak out of me into my panties while we're at the hockey game."

Fuck. My cock jerks inside of her. My hands clamp onto her waist, pulling her down onto my cock as I thrust up into her.

"And later, when we're at the bar with my brother, I want you to pull me into a dark corner and fuck me," she continues. "Hard and fast, barely pulling my pants down long enough to get inside me. It'll have to be quick. You'll pin me against the wall and put your hand over my mouth as you fuck me. We can't be too loud, but I want you to make me scream in that bar so everyone knows what you're doing to me, so everyone knows that I'm yours."

My eyes cross. I want that. I want that so fucking bad. I want to wear her scent like a brand on my skin. I want everyone to know that she's mine and I'm hers and we belong to each other.

"And then you'll pull up my pants with your cum lining the inside of my panties. We're going to go back to our table and you'll shake my brother's hand with my juices on your skin."

"Yes. Please." My cock throbs. "Vivienne, I—"

Her breath hitches as she clenches around me. "Oh, fuck."

"Tell me," I plead. "What happens next?"

"I—I—"

My hand tightens on her hips. "I'll bring you home. I'll draw you a warm bath," I tell her, as my fingers circle her clit. "I'll help you clean up and bring you your book and you'll read out loud to me."

She gasps. "You'd like that?" She swivels her hips and makes me see stars.

"Yeah. I'd like that." I pinch her clit lightly and she clenches around me again, so tight I nearly black out. "And then after, we'll curl up in bed and I'll hold you." My hips punch up. "All. Fucking. Night."

Viv cries out as she comes, her pussy milking my cock. It doesn't take much to push me over the edge and I release into her hot, tight cunt.

Pulling out of her, I roll her onto her back and slide three fingers inside of her, pushing my release deeper inside of her. She lets out a soft moan, twitching around my fingers.

"Tony…"

I kiss her deeply, trying to tell her all the emotions swirling around in my head.

As I slide my fingers out, I bring them to my lips, tasting our combined releases. The salt and musk on my tongue makes my spent cock twitch against her leg, trying to rally.

She lets out a happy sigh, reaching for me. I pull her into my arms and she rests her head on my chest.

"We're going to be okay, aren't we?" She looks up at me with hope in her eyes.

My stomach flips. "Do you have a reason to doubt us?"

"Uh, life?" She waves a hand in the air. "I've never done this. The happy ever after thing."

I kiss her forehead. "Yeah, we're going to be okay."

thirty-three

Viv

THE ARENA IS BUSTLING with the special frenzy of hockey fans. With Tony's hand in mine and Cari beside him, we make our way to the suite we'll be sitting in. As soon as Ceci heard Chuck would be in town, she insisted on coming to the game. Sadie, Vanessa, and Rachel are all in the suite with us, plus what feels like half of our book club. Hailey MacGregor too, whose brother is an assistant captain.

Cari bounds over to Hailey, pulling her into a hug. There are a few other men, mostly the partners of my friends, but the vast majority of our group is female. I love seeing women interested in sports. For so long, it's been such a male-dominated world. I'm glad we're starting to claw our way to an even playing field.

Tony swallows loudly as Ceci approaches with a sharp look in her eyes.

"What's he doing here?" she demands, hands on her hips.

"We like him," I tell her flatly. After all, the last time she'd seen him, I still hated him. Even though we've talked since then, I can't blame her for being wary.

She grins. "Awesome. Welcome to the family, then." Ceci tugs him into a hug.

He looks back at me with wide eyes.

"You'll have to bring your cute friend around sometime," she continues. "I could use more single guy eye candy."

Tony forces a chuckle. "He has a girlfriend."

"Shit. Okay, you're out of the club." She gives him a cheeky smile. "I'm kidding. But make some new, hot friends."

"I'll do my best." He reaches for me, taking my hand. "Thank you for letting us sit with you."

Ceci waves it off. "You're family now."

He's wearing a Gonzales #56 jersey, same as Cari. I pulled out my old Colorado Dragons jersey with Gallagher #12 on the back. If it were any team other than my brother's, I'd have no issue supporting Al.

"Two households, both alike in dignity," Tony murmurs into my ear. "In fair Boston, where we lay our scene."

I laugh. "Okay, Shakespeare. I like to think we'll have a better outcome than Romeo and Juliet."

"Well, if I suddenly appear to have died, check for poison first," he says. "Maybe give it an hour to make sure I'm really dead."

"You won't be pining for the fjords?" I tease.

He shakes his head. "You're mixing your pop culture again."

Drawing him closer, I wind my arms around his neck. "You love it."

"I love *you*." His smile kisses mine. "The rest is just a bonus."

We settle in to watch the game. Since Ceci sprung for a nice suite, we have cushy leather seats instead of the unforgiving plastic stadium seats. Tony holds his own with my friends, but once the game starts, he's laser-focused whenever his brother is on the ice.

I have mixed feelings about who to root for. As much as I want my brother to win, I'm a Boston girl now, and my friends are on the team. Can't I just cheer whenever either side makes a good play?

Alas, it's like Al has rocket fuel in his shakes, because he dekes and fakes out half the Colorado squad before putting a bullet past their goalie. He blows Chuck a kiss and my brother glares at him.

Tomorrow morning, there will be speculation my brother and Tony's brother are in a scandalous relationship. I almost wish it were true. It would certainly fix both of their dating woes. Then at least we'd keep it all in the family.

It sounds like a romance novel. Good thing I know a writer. I make a note to tell Sadie later. Who knows, maybe it will be the plot line of her next book.

The game is exciting, the pace quick as the players get chippy. High in the upper bowl, I can't hear what the players are saying on ice level, but I can see Chuck and Al jawing at each other all game long.

Fuck. I worried so much about me getting along with Tony's siblings, and him getting along with mine, that I didn't consider what would happen if our respective siblings didn't jive.

As if he can sense my agitation, Tony draws his arm around me and pulls me into his side. He kisses my temple and then focuses his attention on the game again.

Rachel and Sadie are across the box. I see them watching me with knowing smirks. I roll my eyes and Rachel outright laughs at me. She's such a little shit.

Last winter, we sat in this arena and watched her now-boyfriend play while she dithered over whether to make a move. I'm the one that convinced her to take the first steps; I claim their relationship as my success.

The score on the ice is tied even, 2-2. Jake Lewis, Rachel's boyfriend, is doing his best to keep the Dragons out of his crease, but the Grizzlies' defense is mediocre at best and pitiful at worst. If it weren't for all of Colorado's shots ending up wide or hitting the post, and if it wasn't for Jake playing the game of his life, the score would be a lot more lopsided.

Chuck has landed four shots on goal, Jake denying him each time. Where I wasn't sure before, now I'm certain: I want my brother to win. At the very least, I want him to score a goal and get the monkey off his back. His hard work and dedication should be rewarded.

I take a few photos of the ice, sending them to the family group chat. Perry sends back a thumbs up and Janine hearts the photo. No response from Frankie or Bradley—yet.

The Dragons score, bringing the tally to 3-2. Boston pulls their goalie to get another attacker on the ice.

And as the final seconds wane, Colorado has the puck. I watch with bated breath as Gibson passes up to Chuck, who stick handles around Al before firing a dart at the net.

4-2 Colorado. Goodnight, Boston.

Understandably, that lets the air out of the crowd's collective sails, but I can't stop smiling.

The sour mood continues as the final buzzer rings and we make our way to the bar. It takes the players a while to do press, shower and change, and leave the arena, so we'll have a good head start on the night by the time they arrive.

Our gang is let into the VIP section by the bouncer and we post up at a few tables. We have a large crowd tonight, not to mention the rest of the players' partners and families. Tony doesn't leave my side, his arm around my waist or his hand holding mine the entire time. When the waiter comes by, he orders us sodas.

"I don't care if you drink," I tell him. "It doesn't bother me."

Just because I'm sober doesn't mean he has to abstain. Sure, I won't like it if he gets blackout drunk, but a few drinks on a night out are not enough to be concerned about in someone who doesn't already have a problem.

I did. I couldn't moderate it. I'm not ashamed of that.

How long it took me to get help, maybe. But if I had gotten help earlier, then I wouldn't have hit my rock bottom when I did, and I wouldn't have had that first night with him. For all the bad that came with it, there was a whole lot of good too.

Tony shrugs. "I don't need to drink tonight. Another time, maybe."

There's a cheer throughout the club, and heads swivel toward the noise. The pack of hockey players have descended upon the place, thundering up the stairs to the VIP section.

To my surprise, there are more than a few Colorado Dragons players mixed with the Grizzlies guys. Al has his arm around Chuck's shoulders. And, even more shocking, Chuck isn't pushing him away.

My brother reaches me and I stand to give him a hug.

"Good game," I yell in his ear. "Congrats on the goal."

"Thanks, V." His eyes skate past me to land on Tony. "So you're the boyfriend."

Tony stands, squaring his shoulders. "Tony Gonzales. Nice to meet you."

Chuck shakes his hand, scrutinizing him. After a moment, he purses his lips and nods. "Okay, I like you."

I laugh. "That's all it took?"

"Nah. *You* like him, so *that* is all it took." Chuck snags a chair and sits. "Tell me. How did you meet? Viv's been fairly quiet in the group chat."

Tony takes my hand. "We met at the Olympics."

"No shit. And you've been dating all this time?"

I shake my head. "His sister joined the Revolution. She actually set me up with Al. That's how I met Tony again."

My brother grins. "And was it love at first sight?"

Laughing, I say, "No."

It's just as Tony opens his mouth and says, "Yes."

Swiveling in my seat, I stare at him. His eyes meet mine resolutely.

"Yes," he says, this time just for me. "It was love at first sight."

My eyes tear up. "I didn't—I was so—"

So mean. So rude. I didn't want to give him an inch, much less a mile.

"I love you," he whispers. "The past is the past. What matters is what we do going forward."

"Retirement," I nod. "Vet school."

Chuck's eyebrows go up. "You're going to vet school? What about rugby?"

"I am," Tony says confidently. "I have to start applying. I'm done with gymnastics after the Olympics. I want to get back there, but after next summer, I'll be done."

"Me too. I'm retiring soon," I admit. "I haven't told Mom and Dad yet. I just… I'm ready to move on."

"Hmm." He sits back in his seat. "Have you thought about what schools you're applying to?"

Tony nods. "I have a few on my list."

"You know, Boulder has one of the best vet schools in the country," Chuck says. "It's not far from Denver, either."

I blink. "How do you know that?"

"Dated a girl who was in vet school. Didn't work out." A sad smile twists his lips.

"She was too smart for you?" I tease.

He has a faraway look in his eye. "Something like that."

"I'll add it to the list," Tony says gamely.

"You would seriously move to Colorado?" I turn to him.

"Chuck and Janine are there. You'd have a support network," he points out.

"Okay, but you'd leave your siblings?"

"They're grown adults. And they'd still have each other." He shrugs. "I don't care where I go to school. If it's a city where you have people, that'll make me feel better. I don't want to uproot your entire life."

"Okay. Let's do it," I decide. I let out a laugh. I can't

believe we're doing this. But I can't imagine doing this with anyone else. I can't imagine *wanting* to do this with anyone other than him.

"Really?" Tony squeezes my hand. "You'd give up your life here in Boston for me?"

It's not my life here. I can visit the city. I can keep in touch with my friends online. Without rugby filling my day, I'll finally have the space to figure out who I am and what I want. Maybe it's taking a more aggressive outreach with social media. Maybe it's advocacy and public speaking. Maybe it's something private and out of the public eye.

Whatever it is, I know I'll have the freedom to explore and navigate it for myself. He gives me the space to mull it over without forcing me to make a decision I'm not ready for.

Wherever we are—in Boston, in Colorado, in freaking Minnesota, I know that I can do anything as long as he's there beside me, cheering me on. Just like I'll always do the same for him.

"Apply to the vet school in Boulder," I tell him. "And if you get in, let's move to Colorado. Together."

Tony cups my cheek, pulling me close for a kiss. He brushes his nose against mine before his lips finally meet mine.

"Together," he whispers.

"Forever."

epilogue

. . .

Tony

THE WARM ATHENS sunlight is no match for the bright lights of the cameras flashing in my face.

"Just smile," Brody mutters to me, his arm around my shoulders. "This is your moment."

Hopefully, my smile doesn't look as forced as it feels as I sling my arm around him and Dylan, another of my teammates on the Olympic roster. After a few weeks of nonstop media attention while at the Games, I'm ready to fade into obscurity again.

My teammates came with me for this semi-final match of Team USA against Australia. Al and my parents are somewhere in the stands, ready to watch Cari and Vivienne kick ass against their bitter rivals. The media isn't done with us though.

Gold medal. We did it. It was close, down to the very last routine. Tommy's excellent pommel horse routine was responsible for launching us into first place.

And then in the final rotation, I nailed my fucking vault, and we won the gold medal.

There are still the individual event finals later this week. I've qualified for both vault and floor exercise. And as much as I want to do my best, as much as I want another medal, I've done what I came here to do.

Last time, the bronze medal felt like a consolation prize rather than a mark of my achievements. Third place in the world felt like a taunt rather than an accomplishment.

Now I've done it. I've hit the pinnacle of success and stuck the landing. Anything after this is just a bonus.

Viv is down on the pitch, ready to play her heart out. She hasn't publicly announced any retirement plans, but Alycia is working hard on a post-Olympics press tour and events. When we went down to South Carolina to tell her parents, her mom cried and her dad went into a planning frenzy on what to do after. Viv took it all in stride, letting them know she was handling it. Well, Alycia is. That counts.

It'll be harder for me to manage, starting vet school three weeks after we get home. I almost deferred the first semester, but it's only a few weeks of craziness. I'll do a few talk shows showing off the gold medal, but I won't go on the full press tour that Viv and Cari will no doubt embark on.

Besides, I'm ready to get started on this next step in my life.

Luckily, we had some help. My mom and Viv's mom were busy at work setting up our new apartment in Boulder, about twenty miles from downtown Denver, where Chuck and Janine live. We had to fly to Greece ahead of time for pre-Games training, so our families took care of packing our boxes, shipping everything, and even had time to start unpacking before they joined us.

Truth be told, I think my siblings are glad I'm moving out. Although we spend a lot of time at Viv's apartment, I don't like to leave Shadow alone too long, so we do spend quite a few nights at the house. And as much as we try to keep things down, Viv isn't known for being quiet.

Taking my seat in the stands, I tug my hat down over my forehead. The sun on my skin does feel nice. After spending the last month training in the gym all day, every day, it's almost a relief to get outside again.

"Cari's looking good out there," Al comments beside me. "Viv too."

"I'll say," Brody says, and I backhand him across the chest.

"Stop perving on my sister. She's too young for you."

My best friend shrugs. "She's hot."

He broke up with his girlfriend about six months ago, right around the time Cari decided she was ready to try wading into the dating pool again. The timing is suspiciously convenient. But I believe him when he says he didn't realize how much he was interested in her until she was suddenly available—and he wasn't. His ex has moved on, so I guess there aren't any bad feelings there. Brody still hasn't actually asked Cari out. I don't know what he's waiting for.

All I know is, it's messy. It's not *my* mess, though. I don't have to worry about it.

Just, like, a little bit of worry. A normal amount. He's my best friend, but she's my sister. I'll always worry about her.

Viv's family is in the row in front of us. All five of her siblings, plus her parents, are here to cheer her on. I've met Mr. and Mrs. Gallagher three times now—they came up to Boston twice, and we went down to South Carolina in March —but I haven't had the opportunity to be with all the siblings at the same time.

When her parents brought Bradley and Frankie up over spring break, they were more interested in seeing the sights than spending time with us. Perry had a football game in the city in December. Janine was kind enough to take us on a tour of the Boulder area when I was touring campus.

To everyone's surprise, Chuck and Al get along like a house on fire. I thought for sure they'd be at each other's throats, but they seem to enjoy riling each other up and then laughing about it after.

I think it might be what Chuck was missing in the distance

from his twin, and what I could never give Al. I don't have the same competitive fire in me. As much as I want to win, gymnastics is all about individual achievements rather than a team working together. Even for a team score, it's about our own efforts.

Being hockey players, Chuck and Al understand each other in a way I never have. I don't feel left out; I'm actually grateful that they've been able to find what they were missing in each other. It's not fun feeling left out.

I didn't realize how alone I was until Viv blasted into my life. I was going through the motions. Training, work, volunteering at the shelter… it consumed me. I didn't hang out with Brody or the guys. I barely saw my siblings…

With the endorsement campaigns Alycia's found for me, I was able to quit my job at the restaurant. Suddenly having twenty hours a week in my schedule means I actually have time to relax and spend time with Viv and my siblings. Separately and together.

"Alright," Mr. Gallagher says, turning around in his seat to face me. "What do you have planned for after this?"

My mouth goes dry. "What do you mean?"

Somehow, I don't think he's talking about where to go for dinner.

"Do I need to start saving up for a wedding?" His walrus-style mustache twitches. I can't tell if that's a good thing.

I think it's a good thing.

"We're not there yet," I tell him honestly. "When she's ready, I'll ask, but we have so much going on in the next year. We need some time for us, first. She needs to figure out what she wants to do after all of this."

"You're not going to string my baby girl along?"

I shake my head. "If I thought she'd say yes, I'd ask her in a heartbeat. Our relationship is too important to me to rush into the next step. We're moving in together, and we're moving halfway across the country to start the next phase of our lives. That's enough life changes for now, I think. We're committed and working toward that, but we're not there yet."

Mr. Gallagher nods. "That's a good rationale."

There's a ring in my duffel bag. I'd kept it in my sock drawer, but since my mom was packing all of my stuff for the movers, I'd brought it with me. I don't have any plans to propose—like I told her dad, I genuinely think we should wait.

But if she even hints about wanting to get engaged, I want to have it on hand. Cari helped me pick it out and Kiana helped me get it sized properly. It was truly a team effort.

Neither of us is ready, but when the time comes, I will be.

On the pitch, Viv and Cari are playing their heart out. Australia is a fierce opponent. There's a reason they've won the last three meetings between the countries. I'm on the edge of my seat as Team USA scores, then the Australians answer back. Every time we go up, they respond immediately.

The score is tied at the half. Viv is focused on the pitch in front of her, all of her attention narrowed in on this game.

This is the end for her. Regardless of the outcome of this game, she's going home a three-time Olympic medalist. The only question is if it's a silver or that elusive gold medal.

And when play resumes, Viv gets the ball back to her teammate. They manage to eke out a score, and then another, and *then* another before Australia is able to catch up.

When the final whistle blows, Viv looks to the stands. There are thousands of people here, but I know she can see me because her smile stretches from ear to ear. She folds her fingers into a heart over her chest, and I do the same. Our super secret-sign language.

And as they place the gold medal around her neck, I cry right along with her, and I don't fucking care who sees it. I'm so proud of her, of everything she's accomplished. It's the perfect way to wrap up her third Olympics, the cherry on top of a storybook career.

This is it. This is the end.

But for us, it's only the beginning.

———

Thank you for reading Ruck Me Harder. I hope you enjoyed the book as much as I enjoyed writing it!

Want to see a peek into the life of Tony and Viv? Get the extended epilogue here.

Falling for the Gonzales family? Check out Al's book, *Power Play*, where he finds a baby on his doorstep... and marries his baby mama's sister to keep custody.

afterword

Thank you for reading *Ruck Me Harder*. This book is my baby and I absolutely love it to pieces.

Reviews are more important than readers realize. If you liked this book, please leave me a review!

<u>Join my newsletter</u> to stay in the loop! Lots of unfunny quips, unsuccessful attempts at wit, and general grouching about the writing process.

xoxo,

Allie

what's next?

Thank you for reading *Ruck Me Harder*.

Want more enemies to lovers? Check out *Tripped Up*. Elsy has hated her best friend's brother since their one night stand thirteen years ago. When she moves to his city, her best friend asks him to take care of her. Oh, and she wants *nothing* to do with him.

For more neurodivergent love stories, check out *The Thought of You*, where Johanna discovers she's autistic when her reformed playboy roommate tells her.

In your hockey era? Check out *Puck Me Twice*, featuring Vanessa and the autistic hockey player she asks to be her fake boyfriend, not knowing he wants it to be real.

about the author

Allie is a queer and AuDHD writer with a hyper-fixation on inclusivity and representation. She loves the color purple, Michigan football, the Detroit Lions, and the Boston Bruins. When she's not absorbed by a book, she likes to spend time with her nephews.

A San Diego, CA native now residing in South Carolina, she is allergic to the cold, rain, snow, and mosquitos.